THE SECRET SISTER
&
THE SILVER KNIGHT

A NOVEL BY

CHRISTINE E. SCHULZE

THE SECRET SISTER AND THE SILVER KNIGHT
CHRISTINE E. SCHULZE
Copyright © 2012 Christine E. Schulze
Cover Art Copyright © 2012 Christine E. Schulze
Drawings Copyright © 2009-2012 Christine E. Schulze
Edited by Joshua R. Shinn
Formatted by Laura Shinn

ISBN: Not Assigned
Self-Published by: Christine E. Schulze 2012
www.thegoldenhealer.blogspot.com

To Sarah, Rachel, Josh, Hailey, Sam, Tiff,
Nathan, and Krystal, as always;

To all my other fellow Bereanians, especially Mrs. Daniels
and her lovely new family;

To Mumsie and Ms. Flem, of course;

To Aaron and Eric, my childhood sweetheart heroes,
and, most importantly, yet good friends;

To Jonny, my new Silver Knight;

And to God for blessing me with you all;
May He bless you all as well.

"Greater love hath no man than this, that a man lay down his life for his friend."
~John 15:13

THE SECRET SISTER

CHAPTER 1

"Chasmira...Chasmira...hey, earth to Cass..."

"Hmm?" Chasmira mused half-absentmindedly. "You say something, Rache?"

"Your history notes. You said I could borrow them, remember?"

"Oh...sure..."

Rachel swiped the notes, sighing as Chasmira's eyes lingered dreamily upon her sole focus, Aaron, who sat a few tables down helping Chryssilla, a new student, with her English assignment.

Though they were now in their Lunar year and an entire year passed since they got together, he still had not asked Chasmira out on a real date. Yet Chasmira remained content. She loved Aaron and finally received his affection in return. For now that seemed more than enough, especially considering she had waited seven years to receive any reciprocation of her feelings at all. She would wait until he was ready to advance further. When you've already been patient for seven years, what do a few more weeks or months really matter?

Chasmira wasn't the only one anticipating a date though. Nathan called Rachel fifty-seven times—she kept thorough tabs—during the summer, in an attempt to ask her out, but this resulted in him either hanging up the phone—which caused Rachel to throw it across the room twice—or stammering so badly she could not make any sense out of what he said.

Josh and Krystal, on the other hand, were "going steady," or as steady as anyone could go with Josh. Their dates always seemed to prove disastrous, usually on Krystal's part, ending with her falling in the mud or receiving skunk-scented perfume. It took a month for her to remove the stench from their last date.

Hailey, Sam, and Sarah remained happily single, though, of course, rumors flew around that Sam and Hailey were in love since they studied so much together. In these cases, Hailey would get annoyed, shrink the gossipers, and put them in a jar for a couple of hours. Once released, they usually never teased Hailey or Sam ever again, nor did they talk to her much at all, glimpsing her with paranoia if they passed in the hall.

Aaron returned to sit by Chasmira, announcing, "Boy, am I starved. Rache, get that chocolate I asked for?"

Rachel shrugged. "Yeah, but Krystal melted it."

"Umm...why...?" His eyes demanded a good explanation of Krystal.

"Don't look at *me*. Rachel's idea..."

"*Rachel...*"

"Dude, you ate chocolate cake two hours ago and threw up all over Professor Miner—*not coolio...*"

"'*Dude.*'" Rachel scowled as he mocked her. "That was *two hours* ago. Remember, you can *never* have too much chocolate—"

"Oh, we are *not* going into that again—"

They nearly jumped out of their seats as the chattering of monkeys loudly sounded.

"What in the world—?" began Sarah.

Josh laughed sheepishly, digging into his pocket. "My cell. Sorry."

Hailey shook her head. "If you're going to have a ringer with animal noises, at least make it something less cliché...like a moose..."

"Hey, Tiff!" Josh greeted into his cell phone. "How's your new school in Texas?"

Aaron's head jerked up, and he frowned. "Texas? Since when does she go to school there?"

Krystal shrugged. "Transferred to some beauty school or the like. Very sudden move, actually..."

"Great—"

"Josh, can I speak to her for a sec?" Krystal asked.

"Sorry, Krys, this is long-distance, and I'm already over my minutes...Yeah, Tiff, Krystal wants to talk to you, but I won't let her...Oh, Tiff says 'Hi.'"

"Tell her I say 'hello.'"

"Yeah, Krystal says 'Hello'...oh, she asks how you're doing."

"I'm doing fine. And herself?"

8

"She's doing fine, and herself—er...yourself? Yeah, I know that was confusing. She just wants to know how you're doing...oh, she's doing 'quite well, thank you,' Krystal."

"This would be so much easier if he just gave me the phone..." mumbled Krystal.

Nathan suddenly materialized a laptop and set it on the table.

Rachel stared, impressed. "Wow. You can materialize more than food now?"

"No, bought it this summer. Just summoned it. I'll be taking computer courses for the next three years, so I figured I may as well get one..."

"Hey," said Josh, finally off the phone. "If you ever *do* figure out how to materialize computers, you know where to find me..."

"Oh, you don't *need* one," Krystal retorted then turned to Rachel. "Nathan's already got him hooked on Lunescape, that bloody RPG..."

"Oh, for Jiminy cricket's sake," Rachel groaned.

"So, did anyone hear from Eric this summer?" Sam asked.

Aaron shrugged. "Nope." Everyone else concurred the same.

Josh shook his head. "Lucky dude, getting to go on secret missions, skipping school...never tells me about them either..."

"Umm...they're secret?" Krystal suggested in her *I hate to state the obvious* tone.

At the mention of Eric's name, Chasmira began fumbling with the jade-green bracelet Eric had left in her care before his departure. She wore it all the time, taking good care of it, fulfilling her promise. Its presence often reminded her to pray for him as well, made her wonder what he was doing, where he was...

"Hey, that bracelet looks familiar," mused Rachel. "My sister had a blue one just like it. Where'd you get it?"

"Eric gave it to me before he left. Said it was his sis—wait, you had a sister too?"

"Yeah, she was a very gifted fairy, beautiful, smarter than me even! And then she mysteriously disappeared..."

"Hold those thoughts, people, gotta potty." Josh jumped up from the table. All ignored him, save Krystal who faithfully rolled her eyes.

Aaron leaned over the table, eyes growing more curious and suspicious. "Sounds like what happened to my sister."

"Sylvia?" asked Chasmira, starting. "She's missing too?"

"Well, you haven't seen her since you came here, have you?"

"Well, no, but I assumed she was almost done with college so we just never see her, but why didn't you tell me about this before?"

Aaron shrugged. "Every time my family and I tell people Sylvia just vanished, they look at us like we have ten heads or something. It *is* weird though. She went on some special, secret mission and never returned."

"That's what happened to Barbara!" exclaimed Rachel. "Aaron, did Sylvia have a bracelet too?"

Aaron screwed up his face into a deep-thinking expression. "Yeah! A yellow one. She wouldn't let *anyone* touch it. I don't think she even took it off in the shower. I just figured her boyfriend gave it to her or something..."

Chasmira fiddled nervously with the green bracelet. "So what do you think it all means?"

"Dunno, but I say we read into it," said Rachel.

"Like, go to Mr. Root or something?" suggested Hailey.

"Uhh, no. No sense in bringing a teacher into something we don't even know necessarily means a big deal, and besides, most of them are off at the teacher's conference this week. Just a bunch of subs left. No, I mean *literally* read into it. To the library!"

CHAPTER 2

Sarah Schnur was hot, and she knew it. She knew it because all the guys on campus knew it and constantly proceeded to stare, gawk, follow her around like shameless, lost puppies, or nonchalantly—she hoped—ask for her hand in marriage. Thus, Sarah often wished she did not know she was hot.

She was wishing this very thing as she and Joshua, a boy in her class that looked uncannily like Josh White, mohawk and all, save he was taller, finished tidying up the science lab. Everyone else disappeared for lunch long ago, leaving Sarah to clean up the remainder of the uncertain, neon-green, gooey substance that someone—Sarah guessed it was Caleb—managed to splatter on every inch of the room. Joshua volunteered to help, and it seemed to Sarah that he scrubbed the same spot on the wall uncommonly slowly for the past ten minutes, so much so that every time his magic scrub brush circled, it squeaked. It squawked rhythmically as he looked up at her for the zillionth time, flashing an annoyingly handsome yet somehow dorky smile. One of those guys who *knew* he was cute to nearly every girl that passed by. Definitely on Sarah's long "don'ts" list.

Suddenly, a siren began to whir, and Joshua announced, "That's the intruder drill siren."

"So, what's the procedure?" Sarah asked.

"Standard is to turn off the lights and hide in the closet." He strolled over towards the light switch.

"You're joking," she scoffed, staring at him.

"Nope," he returned, calmly and seriously.

The lights clicked off, leaving only a very dim glow shining through the blinds drawn almost completely taut. Enough light remained for her to see him scrambling in the closet, and, despite the siren's continual whirring, she could hear him yell out as he bumped against something. She would've snickered but could only sigh and mumble irritably to herself as she made her way to the closet, and jumped inside. As he closed the door, she pressed herself as tightly as possibly against the far corner, which was, unfortunately, not very far from him at all. She could see the glint of Joshua's eyes as the siren's blare spiraled to a stop. He produced a small orb of light that hovered dully between them. Then he smiled with suave cheesiness.

"Cozy in here, ehh?"

"Can we leave?" she hissed.

"No, I think we're supposed to wait for further instruction."

Sarah opened her mouth to assure him that leaving this closet was the only way to spare him from further *pain*, when the door burst open and someone shoved inside.

"Sarah!"

She groaned. It was Nate Fischer from English. *Oh, the horror.*

She glared at him as he panted, breathing all over her. Then, his eyes fell upon Joshua.

"Vhat are you doing in here vith my leetle lemone drop?" Nate hissed, narrowing his eyes dangerously at Joshua while sticking out his bottom lip in a not-at-all-attractive sort of pout. Sarah thought that, altogether, the effect of the face made him look like a pug wearing a beret.

Sarah glared at him more than skeptically, pressing herself even more tightly against the not-nearly-deep-enough-for-her-liking back wall of the closet, secretly hoping that by some miracle or random prank of Josh White's she would sink into it and fall out the other side into another room, or, for Pete's sake, another dimension even.

"Umm, I am *not* your lemon drop any more than I am wanting to be shoved into this tiny closet with you two breathing into and therefore majorly invading my personal bubble."

The door opened yet again, and someone else fell in.

"Whoa, dude, heh, heh, like, there's a lot of people in here—"

"Josh White, you had so better have a good reason—"

"Well, there was, like, that drill, so I was rushing to find a closet because that's what Lucy said you should do if we ever heard the siren—"

"Lucy?" Sarah echoed, rolling her eyes. "The one hot after Nathan?" Oh, now she was sure the closet thing had been a scam...

"Well, she's apparently hot after me now, and, while I admit to my utter hotness, well, she was all chasing after me, it was sort of creepy-like, and this was the first closet I came to, so I was making a dive for it before she caught me, I mean, I am with Krystal, gotta make a good reputation for myself and stuff now —"

Footsteps reverberated in the room, and Sarah felt Josh clutch her legs, trembling. "Aww, man, she found me, *aww, man—*"

Sarah was preparing to kick him very hard when the lights clicked on, the door shot open, and standing there was—

"Mike, thank Amiel," she sighed. It was Mike from History, the only normal guy standing in the room and therefore, at this moment, her hero.

"Umm...what's going on?" He glanced weirdly at the scene which Sarah knew must be comical to any outsider. She was shoved in a corner, Josh kneeling and clutching her legs like he was hanging on for his life, Nate and Joshua scrunched at the other side of the closet like they were about to make out...eww, scratch that last awful, mental image...

"Intruder drill," Sarah mumbled, wriggling away from Josh and stumbling out of the closet.

Mike caught her and set her aright. "Umm...and you didn't head to the dining hall why?"

"Because some people are apparently confused and thought we were supposed to hide in a closet." She glared sharply at Joshua while Nate exclaimed, "Fiend! I knew you vere trying to deceive my leetle lemone drop for your deerty purposees!"

Mike laughed. "How in the world would we all fit inside closets?"

Josh chortled. "Good point, my good man, good point."

"Look." Sarah took in a deep breath, trying very hard to remain at least a little bit calm. "I know this is all very amusing to all of you, but if we could leave now, I have not had a bite to eat for lunch—"

"You want me to escort you to the dining hall?" Mike asked.

Sarah glanced at Nate and Joshua, both staring at her like hopeful prospects.

"Sure, Mike, that'd be really great."

"Okay then. M'lady."

He held out his arm, and as she linked hers in his, Nate muttered, "I shall vin your heart still, my leetle lemone drop," while Josh exclaimed, "Dude! Like, your name's 'Josh' too? That's, like, totally awesome. Sweet mohawk, man. Heh, heh, reminds me of a cool one I saw one other dude wear once..."

Sarah shook her head, and once they were a considerable distance away from the room, Mike took the liberty to burst out laughing.

"Well, I'd like to have seen that one play out."

"I told you I attract all the weirdoes," Sarah mumbled, attempting to glare at Mike as he chuckled, but his blue eyes twinkled so perfectly she couldn't help relaxing and smiling herself. "It will make a good story to tell later..."

"Indeed."

"And at least you were there to rescue me—for the second time this week."

"Indeed again..."

As they rounded the corner, the dining hall looming into view, Chasmira, Aaron, Rachel, Nathan, Sam, Hailey, and Krystal all poured from within.

"Hey, guys, done with lunch already?" Sarah called.

"Yup, heading to the library—important business," Rachel replied.

"Aww, man," Sarah muttered.

"You know, I can save you a spot at one of the lunch tables if you wanna go check out whatever they're doing," Mike said.

"You haven't eaten yet?"

"Nah, I was working on...science project."

Sarah studied him doubtfully. She was good at telling when people lied. He was horrible at hiding the truth. Still, it was sweet, and she liked Mike. Besides, she might need him as a shield against Nate and Joshua should they pop up again, which they undoubtedly would at some point or other. "Sure, that'll be great."

"Okay, see you then."

As he waved and headed into the dining hall, Sarah raced up to the others.

Rachel's eyes sparkled playfully. "And who was he?"

"Just Mike from history."

"'*Just* Mike from history.' Uh-huh. That's what they *all* say..."

"Don't get started, Rachel..."

"Hey, no chance you saw Josh anywhere, eh?" Krystal asked Sarah. "He went to the bathroom about fifteen minutes ago."

"Oh, trust me, I saw more of Josh than I ever care to see again."

Krystal stared at her in an *oh, dear, what has he done this time* fashion, but Sarah only sighed and shook her head. "I'll have to tell you all about it later. So, what's this library business?"

Rachel explained quickly about the bracelets.

Sarah narrowed her eyes pensively. "Hmm...sounds fishy to me...especially if Eric's involved with one of the bracelets..."

"Why do you say that?" Hailey asked.

"Well, he always *was* mysterious-like, you know—"

"Aww, man, that is so true."

Sarah groaned as Josh rejoined them, and Krystal glared sharply at him as he linked his arm in hers.

"What?" he cried innocently. "What am I in trouble for this time?"

"I don't know yet," Krystal muttered in a tone that assured she would know soon enough.

They climbed to the top floor of the building where the college library sprawled before them like a sea filled with unknown trials. And, indeed, each book, each page would be a carefully-examined treasure map as they searched for the words they sought, the wisdom that might reveal the truth about the bracelets.

"Where to?" Aaron stopped, Chasmira beside him, along with everyone else.

"Magic section?" Nathan hinted. "Search for something on magical items?"

Aaron shrugged. "Let's get to it."

They each split up, trickling into different aisles, some *too* different. Hailey had to shrink Sam just to get his attention as he became enthralled in a book about the legendary time-traveling herbs. Once returned to his original size, he blushed sheepishly, apologizing, though she assured him it was alright. Anyone might turn astray upon locating such a find.

They'd been searching hardly ten minutes when Josh strolled casually into the row where Sarah stood, carefully flipping through and scanning pages of a huge volume. He sauntered a bit *too* casually, whistling with hands shoved in pockets. While she rolled her eyes inwardly, she kept focused on the task before her. Until he stood behind her, breathing loudly and hotly, and she snapped the book shut, smirking as he choked on the cloud of dust rising up.

As he coughed, she assumed herself victorious and began to walk away 'til she heard, "And *vhat* are you doing, annoying my leetle lemone drop?"

She cringed. She froze. She turned.

"What do you want, Nate? Why are you following us around?"

He smiled, leaning his shoulder towards the bookshelf in a "cool" stance. His shoulder missed, and he nearly toppled over but caught himself with one hand and stood awkwardly, still smiling. His beret now cocked to one side, covering one eye. "I saw you all comeeng up to thee libraree, and I said to myself, 'My leetle lemone drop looks as though she is on an important miss-ee-own, so perhaps I can be of 'elp.' Can I 'elp you, my leetle lemone drop?"

Sarah sighed. At least, this time, it would be easy to get rid of him.

"Yes. We're looking for something on magical bracelets. One yellow, one blue, one green. They all look the same except for the color."

"I am on thee case! My leetle lemone drop."

He raised his brows and winked at her before strutting to the next aisle.

"Heh, heh, little lemon drop." Josh smirked, prepared to elbow her playfully, but a quick glare told him she would *not* be playing if he even *considered* touching her.

Josh walked off wisely, leaving Sarah to her flipping.

After several more minutes of bliss, the shout resounded, "I 'ave found eet! I 'ave found thee mageek braceleets! I 'ave found eet!"

Everyone rushed towards the sound of Nate's excited cries.

Sarah muttered, "Oh, you have *got* to be kidding..."

As soon as they all clustered around Nate who held the book open, eyes gleaming, Rachel muttered, "Who's *this* character?"

Aaron laughed. "I thought you were doing your 'French herb' impressions again, Sam."

Sam drew himself up proudly and returned in an offended tone, "My French herb dialect is much more advanced than that, good monsieur."

"So this is Nate, he's in one of my classes, yadda, yadda, we're all glad to meet you, Nate. What did you find?"

"I found theese."

He held up the book, showing it to all. Gasps raced amongst them.

"That's it," Chasmira breathed, glancing from the book to her own bracelet and back again. "That's exactly like it."

"What's it say, other Nathan?" Nathan chuckled at his own bad humor while Rachel only made a face and shook her head in shame.

"Eet says, 'Thee four eleemental braceleets vield thee pow-airs of snow, veend, rain, and fi-air. They are von-of-a-kind, extremely powerful items whose pow-airs should not be undairestimated.'"

He looked up.

"That's it?" Chasmira asked.

He nodded. "Zat ees eet."

"Man, that whomps," Josh snorted.

Rachel shrugged. "But at least we know more about them now."

"And why my sister and Rachel's sister disappeared," added Aaron.

They all stared at him curiously.

"*Come on.*" He rolled his eyes. "It should be obvious to us by now. Powerful, magical item, one-of-a-kind—"

"Someone's looking for them, trying to collect them all," surmised Chasmira.

"Exactly." Aaron gazed at her with all seriousness. "Which is why you will go nowhere unattended."

She stared. "*What?*"

"I don't want anything happening to you."

"Aaron—"

"Even *I* have to agree with him on this one," Sarah concurred. "I mean, if some crazy dude's out there looking for the thing..."

"At least we know it's not Rorrim this time," muttered Rachel.

"Yes, and at leest I can rest assured it ees not my leetle lemone drop that is in dangeair." Nate drew an arm around Sarah's waist too firmly for her to break away. She could only stand there awkwardly, rigid, fuming, as he whispered in her ear, "I feel your ten-see-own, my leetle lemone drop. Do not vorree. I shall protect you."

She inwardly mused how *he* would not be protected as soon as they were alone together again if he did not let go *very quickly*...

"Just...I mean...don't go wandering around the garden or somewhere alone, okay, Cassy?"

She looked up into Aaron's serious, imploring eyes. She couldn't help but smile. Overprotective. Yet wasn't this the kind of attention she craved from him? It would give them more excuses to be together, allow her to hang it over his head if he said he didn't feel like walking her to class that day or if he forgot to meet her somewhere.

"I promise."

He sighed, relieved.

"Well, now that's done, let's go play some four-square or something, ehh?"

"You guys have fun. I gotta go catch me some lunch." Sarah wrenched away from Nate's grasp.

"Vould you like for me to come vith you, my leetle lemone drop?"

"No, I wouldn't," she called back, her reserve of patience and tact all spent, veiled by her grumbling hunger.

"Alvight, my leetle lemone drop! I shall see you in class after lunch!"

She groaned, suddenly thinking she needed to go on an eating spree that lasted through her next several classes.

CHAPTER 3

Sarah's day started quite nicely the next morning. Mike invited her to have breakfast with him, and he shared a lovely rumor that Nate was sick. There should be no interruptions from him that afternoon.

Aaron entered the dining hall scanning it for any signs of his friends, one in particular. The discoveries of yesterday thrust him into a sleepless, thought-filled night. He *must* overcome his fear of relationships, and now was as good a time as any. Having to protect Chasmira was certainly one, good reason to ease himself back into the whole dating business. Besides, if she stuck around for him this long without them actually even dating, she wouldn't say "no," right? After all, she was just as committed to him as he was, in his heart, to her.

Espying Hailey and Sam, he walked over to their table.

"Hey, have you guys seen Chasmira?"

"Shh," hissed Hailey sharply, not allowing her gaze to stray. Sam too seemed transfixed upon something. It was Sarah and Mike.

"Umm, what're we doing here?" Aaron asked, perplexed.

Hailey grinned mischievously. "It's like watching a soap opera."

"Very entertaining," added Sam.

"Yes, but what exactly are we watching?"

"Sarah's met someone," Sam said.

"Well, good for her? I met at least three people today—"

"She's met *a guy*."

At these words, Aaron too turned and stared. But then he remembered his own mission and snapped out of the beginning reverie.

"Seriously, guys, have you seen Chasmira? I need to ask her something."

"Oh, she went towards the theatre," Hailey snapped irritably before sinking back into her enthralled state of ogling.

Aaron made his way to the theatre, deciding he would sneak in quietly. She was probably practicing for her performance in the upcoming fall play. She *never* let him watch her practice, said it distracted her and made her blush. He smirked. As if *every*thing didn't make her blush in his presence. As if he didn't like it that way. As if her constant blushing didn't give him the courage to tell her what he wanted to tell her now...

He reached the theatre and slipped noiselessly in. She stood on stage with a single, heavenly light shining down upon her. Aaron took a seat in the very top row, hidden in the shadows, though he could have turned invisible, had he willed it. But she would be far too immersed in her performance to have a chance of seeing him.

She beamed radiantly, like some mysterious, celestial being, as she performed an act from "The Enchantress." It was one of the plays he wrote and just published over the summer. Chasmira played the young girl who won the dark enchantress' hatred by murdering her brother, who himself had been a dark wizard.

Chasmira suddenly drew silent and turned towards the left of the stage. Then she walked slowly towards that side. She was supposed to be in a trance at this part, and she was certainly doing a very good job of acting it out.

Yet as she continued to walk, spell-bound, he frowned. This wasn't in the script. Someone was supposed to enter the room, and she was supposed to wheel around, snapping out of the trance. And where was that mysterious melody drifting from? It sounded sort of like the chimes of a music box.

Chasmira continued her slow, steady pace towards the left of the stage, and Aaron began to worry. It was then he noticed—something upon her arm glimmered a vivid green, its glow brightening as she stepped further towards the left of the stage. *The bracelet!* He leapt from his seat, flying down the aisle.

"Chasmira, stop!" he shouted desperately, as loud as possible. For a moment, she hesitated, but then walked on.

"Cassy, *please!*"

She was nearly behind the curtain now, almost to the strange green light radiating from behind it, matching the bracelet's poisonous shade.

Aaron raced as fast as his legs would take him. He was nearly there and could see her eyes, the pupils contracted to mere dots, transfixed, enthralled, captivated by whatever darkness led her on. He clambered up on stage, rushed to her, grabbed her arm, flung her around—

The green light vanished, and Chasmira immediately came around, blinking in confusion.

"What...happened...?"

"You were in a trance," Aaron breathed shakily, holding firmly to her arm as if fearing she would start wandering off again at any moment.

"Oh, yes," she whispered slowly. "I heard this music. It was so peaceful, and at the same time...frightening. It was frightening because I couldn't stop. I just kept following it. I was drawn to it. It was like being in a trance because I couldn't stop, and yet, not like a trance because I knew what I was doing..."

"It was the bracelet. It was glowing. Chasmira, I think you should take it off. It's clearly dangerous."

"But Eric entrusted it to me—"

"Something's *not right* about that bracelet!"

Chasmira looked at him helplessly. She knew he yelled out of frustration, out of concern for her safety, not because of anger. Yet she could do nothing to comfort him, only return in a fearful whisper, "Aaron, I *can't*. I've already tried, after our discussion yesterday. It *won't* come off, there's something wrong with it."

Aaron stared, first at Chasmira, then at the wretched thing with disgust and contempt.

"Perhaps another must take it off for you." He held a very small hope the answer was so easy.

And, indeed, it proved not that simple. Hard as he tried, the bracelet would not budge from her wrist.

"Alright." Aaron released a deep sigh. "We know we can't go to the library for more assistance, and most of the teachers are gone this week for conference. That leaves only one other option."

Chasmira looked at him curiously, prompting him to continue.

"It's time we paid a visit to Amanda Danielle."

CHAPTER 4

Everyone clutched hands tightly as Chasmira shouted, "To Amanda Danielle!"

She and Aaron told the rest of the group about the enchantment of the bracelet and all agreed that whisking themselves away through a space warp to seek council from one of their favorite teachers was the only solution to engage in for now. And so whisk themselves away they did. Even Mike came along for the ride, half because he didn't wish to tear himself from Sarah, half because he really felt curious and wanted to help, if he could.

They landed in the midst of the garden where Amanda Danielle knelt, carefully inspecting her roses, watering can in hand.

She looked up, smiling at them. "Well, good to see you all, and, for once, it's not in the middle of the night when all good students should be snuggled in their beds, dreaming of the morrow's classes. In fact..." She narrowed her eyes. "Shouldn't you all be in class right about now?"

"Uhh, we're all on break." Aaron hoped this was true for all, though if it wasn't, it didn't seem utterly important at the time. "We have a problem. We need your help, your advice, something."

"Unc Josh! Unc Josh!"

A little boy and a little girl with golden, rainbow-streaked hair tottered into the clearing, the girl giggling with outstretched arms, the boy shouting, "Unc Josh!" at the top of his tiny lungs. Josh crouched down and caught them both in a huge hug as they catapulted into his arms, and then little Cooper began to press Josh's nose like a button and declare with delighted triumph, "Got yo no'! Got yo no'!"

"Heh, heh, little imps, gotta love 'em," Josh laughed.

Toby rushed into the clearing, bending over and panting.

"Sorry, dear, they got away again," he gasped guiltily at Amanda Danielle. She only smiled.

"Hmm...perhaps you can satisfy them with a snack while I have a chat with my students here."

"Hi, guys." He raised his hand in a feeble wave before sneaking up on the twins from behind, scooping them up, and, after reassuring them, he carried them towards a mountain of ice cream, and proceeded to make different animal noises while Cooper began to poke his nose, exclaiming "Got dada no'!" Mirabel giggled and clapped her hands in delight.

Josh sighed as he stood. "Heh, ain't they cute?"

"Hmm, dunno," smirked Krystal. "Cooper's rather starting to take after *you*."

"Heh, heh, I know—*hey...*"

"They're beautiful kids, Mrs. Daniels," said Mike.

"Why, Michael Phoenix! What are you doing here with the 'normal' group?"

Hailey rolled her eyes. "He's with Sarah."

"Which means he's officially not normal anymore," Aaron whispered to Nathan, who snorted while Sarah glared.

"I see." Amanda Danille's own eyes sparkled as they trailed to Sarah's and Mike's linked hands. Then, a grave shadow passed over those blue-violet spheres. "Now, about this advice you seek? It is important, I hope, seeing as some of you missed class to come here."

"How *does* she know?" Nathan hissed.

"It's about this," Aaron gently led Chasmira forth, and holding up the wrist where the bracelet dangled, glittering innocently, he told her what they discovered of the bracelet and of the eerie trance that fell upon Chasmira while wearing it.

After the brief explanation, Amanda Danielle stood frowning, eyes serious with intense pensiveness. "And there is no one else you could have told? Mr. Root, perhaps?"

Aaron shook his head. "Mr. Root, Pastyre Saltzgiver, Mrs. Labrier—they're all on conference this week."

She stood silent for a few moments, eyes flashing with concentrated contemplation. Finally, she looked up. "I too have heard of these elemental bracelets, though I know no more about them than yourselves.

"But as for counsel, what I can tell you is this. Whoever seeks to find them, as it seems obvious someone does, and wants them very badly indeed to locate them in the first place, seeing as they are one of a kind. Therefore, if they seek them so desperately, there is a good chance that they know most of the teachers are gone on conference, that you cannot seek their aid or council. And so, I would say this—be about your guard, above all times during this week, especially while all authorities are absent. During this week too would I watch Chasmira closely, just as you have suggested, Aaron."

He nodded. "Thanks."

"I am sorry I can offer no more help."

"It's okay. Thanks again."

"You're welcome." Her smile softened. "And now, if you'll please excuse me, I must see who is winning the battle inside the castle—my husband, the children, or the ice cream."

She turned to leave but paused long enough to add, "If danger befalls you, you know where to find me."

As soon as she slipped from sight, Josh sighed. "Guess that's it."

"Wasn't a total loss," Rachel said. "At least we realize just how careful we need to be, I mean, she made some good points. Good chance we're up against a whack just as crazed as Rorrim."

Aaron's eyes flickered doubtfully. "Yeah, let's not think about that for now though. Nothing bad has happened. Everything's okay. Let's just get back before Mrs. Daniels has a fit about us missing another class or something."

They all held hands once more and soon stood within the confines of the phoenix clearing. Everyone began to file in their separate directions, but Aaron held Chasmira's hand firm. She looked up at him curiously, and he nodded ever so slightly towards the others. Understanding, she held back until they cleared out and the two stood alone in their special place.

"What is it, Aaron?"

"When I came searching for you in the theatre, Cassy, I meant to ask you something..."

His voice trailed. He instantly regretted the words. Yet as soon as he spoke them her eyes shone with such a shimmering hope, just as they did every time he told her he wanted to talk to her. A part of his heart said to wait for a safer time, but the other half of his heart tore at its own heart strings. How could he refuse those glittering, hope-filled spheres yet again? And when would a safer time come? He had a feeling that could be a while. He felt too that if he refused those eyes too many times, their glitter might someday extinguish completely, and it would be his fault...

"Chasmira, would you like to go out on a date with me this Saturday? Nothing fancy, we could do something here at school, the garden even—"

She took in a sharp breath, beaming as she threw her arms tightly around him, choking him almost, though he didn't mind. He held her close. He made a good choice. This felt right, her in his arms, her joy radiating, flowing into him as he clutched her yet more tightly to him. It made him think that everything would be okay, because, in this moment, everything was perfect.

CHAPTER 5

Nathan released a deep sigh. "Okay, major problem. I asked Rachel on a date for Saturday."

"Me too. I mean, I asked Krystal," Josh added quickly, after Nathan cast him a sharp glare.

"Yes, and Hailey and I are having an outing that night," quipped Sam.

Nathan rolled his eyes. "Can't you just call it a 'date?'"

"How many times must I tell you that we're not dating? We're *just* friends," Sam replied irritably.

"Whatever—"

"So, what's the problem?" asked Aaron. "I'm going out with Chasmira that night, and I'm rather elated, personally."

Nathan's shoulders slouched dismally as if he awaited the world's end. "We don't know what to do—where to take the girls."

"Well..." Aaron said slowly, thinking. "I'm taking Chasmira on a picnic to the phoenix clearing. Perhaps you could all pick a special spot in the garden and do the same."

The guys considered the matter then nodded.

"That sounds good," agreed Nathan.

"I was also thinking we could stay fairly close together," added Aaron. "You know, in case something goes wrong, like Chasmira entering into one of those weird trance things again. Although, it would be nice if you all could keep it a secret, you know, we all decide in advance where exactly in the garden we're taking each of our dates. Chasmira will get annoyed if she realizes how big a deal I'm making out of keeping her safe."

"Hey, admitting it is the first step," Nathan teased.

"No problem," agreed Sam, and Josh nodded.

"Cool. Then everything's settled."

* * *

Everything but one thing, Aaron thought. *And I'd rather throw myself off a hundred-foot bridge than do it.*

It was true that Aaron and Krystal never got along very well, and asking her for help might not seem the wisest plan Aaron ever devised. Yet for now, it remained his only option. Saturday arrived already, and he hadn't been able to contrive any other solutions for how to obtain what he so desired to include in his "perfect" date. For it *must* be perfect. It was their first date, his and Chasmira's. And she *was* Chasmira. That simple fact alone created a deserving enough requirement of a perfect date.

As he approached Krystal, scribbling away irritably in her journal, he groaned inwardly. Her clearly sour expression turned even more sour as he approached.

"Hey, Aaron." She cast a pathetically attempted half-smile.

"Hey," he mumbled.

An uncomfortable silence followed. Finally, Krystal's hand grew rigid, and she lay down the pen.

"Alright, Aaron, what do you want? And make it something simple because Josh is taking me out tonight, and I have enough to worry about. Last time he nearly shrank my ears off."

"Don't worry, it'll be simple enough. I'm also taking Chasmira on a date tonight and I was wondering if you could do something to help me out." *There, I asked her.*

Krystal stared at him as though he were insane. "You're asking *me* for help?"

"Look, if you won't do it for me, do it for Chasmira, okay?"

"Fine. But, like I said, Josh is taking me out too."

"Oh, our date's in the garden, so that won't be a problem."

Krystal eyed him suspiciously. "How do you know Josh is taking me to the garden?"

"Uhh...beside the point." Aaron diverted her squinting, piercing eyes. "Anyhow, I was hoping to take advantage of your mad fire skills and use them for a more positive purpose, you know, like making us some fireworks." He paused. Her eyes did not squint any further, but he still wasn't sure he was actually gaining himself any points. "Perhaps you could be there at say...nine o'clock? We'll be in the phoenix clearing."

For a while, Krystal just sat staring as though she might literally burn a pit of ashes through his heart at any moment. How he *hated* when she did this. Couldn't she just answer a person?

Finally, she agreed, "Sure. What did you have in mind?"

He heaved a huge, relieved sigh.

"Well..."

CHAPTER 6

Aaron led Chasmira, in his familiarly handsome blue sweater, into the familiarly special clearing with the lofty tree where the phoenix nest once rested.

He laid the blanket on the ground and together they sat beneath the tree. Aaron opened the basket and began taking out all sorts of food. Chasmira knew it must be a magic basket because the mound of stuff would never fit in a normal basket.

He presented fancy plates and glasses, candles that lit themselves as soon as they were set on the candelabrum, and Nathan, who of course could supply almost endless amounts of food out of thin air, provided food for all the guys' dates, in this case, lasagna and chocolate cake, two of her favorites.

"Nate did a *great* job with the food," Aaron commented.

"Hmm...*you* did a great job overall yourself." Chasmira smiled and blushed radiantly at him.

"Thanks." Smirking, he acknowledged his own blushing, supposing he would have to get used to that now with him taking Chasmira on dates and all. She was more than worth the bit of embarrassment accompanying the blushing. She was more than worth many things...

Finding himself staring at her, he suddenly realized the reason for her very intense flushing as she glanced awkwardly from him to the ground to the food. Breaking away his gaze, he muttered, "Uhh, let's say grace and eat."

Aaron prayed then set about serving Chasmira, who thanked him timidly. He smiled, for every little thing he did to show her attention seemed to send her beaming and blushing with a sincere fervor. How blessed he was to have someone who loved him that much...

"Ahh." As the memory struck him, he dug into the pocket of his khaki pants. His hand emerged, fist tightly concealing something. "Got you something."

She took in her breath, eyes glittering like an anticipating child.

"Close your eyes."

She did so, and a fire rushed through her every fiber right to the core of her heart as he took her right hand, placing something over it and upon her wrist. Letting go, he whispered, "Open now."

29

She did, looking down and staring wonderingly. It was a beautiful, golden bracelet containing tiny diamonds glittering with rainbow facets.

"They're meg-flower diamonds, after your birthday gem. I know how much you like stones and gems and such anyways, and I know how you like, umm, keep-sakes of people. So I thought you might, you know, like—"

"I *love* it, Aaron," she said quietly and with all the sincerity in the world, hugging him close.

While Aaron and Chasmira enjoyed their first bit of official romance, Nathan led Rachel to the garden's small waterfall.

"So, umm," he was saying nervously for the twentieth time in the past five minutes. He spoke the two syllables more and more frequently as they neared their destination. Rachel did not fail to keep count nor to note their frequency as the date progressed. After all, they were all signs of Nathan's sweetness and timidity, and she must record such things in her heart so she could treasure them for a long time to come.

The only other words she pulled from him when she tried to make conversation were, "Umm, yeah," and "I think," and something indecipherable that sounded like "ergle-york." As she could not think of any words in the English dictionary which correlated with this word, she just shrugged it off, reminding herself to come up with her own definition later.

He led her across the stepping stones of the small lake the waterfall poured gently into, tripping so much that Rachel more or less led him. They slipped behind the fall to the small alcove behind where he already set up the picnic dinner before their arrival. This was just as well, considering the fact he felt so nervous that he would have been likely to materialize some mysterious herb that even Sam and Hailey would not dare to eat. Rachel looked about wonderingly as the candle-light scintillated upon the wall of water which cascaded like glittering diamonds, concealing them from all the rest of the world. Just her and Nathan. She beamed at him.

"Ehh, you like all of it?"

A complete sentence. She smiled larger still. "It's all beautiful, Nathan."

"Glad to hear it. Umm, sit and eat?"

He motioned awkwardly with a quivering hand. He was so adorable when he was awkward.

As she sat beside him, he exclaimed, "Oh! Forgot you something."

He reached into the small basket beside him and pulled out—

"A book!" she squealed, taking it into her hands. "Oh, Nathan, and it's the two hundred and third volume in the *Dragon Legends Series*, my favorite! Oh, Nathan, thank you!"

She kissed him, and he fainted dead way into the apple cream pie. Rachel only smiled and hugged her book to her chest, a thousand different methods of how she might preserve the jacket cover racing through her mind. She thought dreamily how truly cute he looked when he fainted into apple cream pie.

CHAPTER 7

Sarah stood in the hall outside her dorm room door, waiting anxiously, heart and stomach quivering with excitement, when her ears perked up. Footsteps. She smiled.

He rounded the corner. She frowned. *He* was not, in any way, shape, or form, Mike.

"Ahh, my leetle lemone drop! How ees eet you are up and alone at such an hoair?"

"Umm...how is it you are meandering the girls' dorms?"

"Ah, hee, hee, my lemone drop! You 'ave caught me. I 'ave come seeking your hand een, vhat do you call, ehh, a courting reetual."

"Umm...I'm really sorry, Nate, but I'm already engaging in, what do you call, a *date*, tonight with Mike."

"Mike?" Nate narrowed his eyes. "Who do you speak of, theese Mike fellow?"

"Uhh...he's the one that rescued me from Josh in the closet."

Nate sighed. "An honorable fellow, at least 'ee 'as proveen. Vell, my leetle lemone drop, eef you think you vill be 'appy with 'im—"

"Quite."

"—I give you your freedom. But know that eef your heart should de-sigh-air to return to me, that my heart is evair beating for you, and you alone, my leetle lemone drop."

He smiled reassuringly before slipping around the corner. Sarah smiled at him as sincerely as she could—which was to say the smile really was not sincere at all, save her sincere elation in his departure—as he glided from view.

Only moments later, a new set of footsteps approached. She tensed with instant panic, thinking this had *so* better be Mike. But, alas, she soon heard, accompanied with the clicking heals, a wailing moan. "Joshy, oh my Joshy-pu, where hast thou forsaken me to? Oh, where can he be, my Joshy-pu?"

Sarah wondered if there were any rules at all whatsoever anymore about boys and girls staying away from each other's quarters, feeling quite insecure about the possibility of Josh roaming her corridors. She reminded herself that at least if Josh and Nate were allowed to sneak down here, so could Mike, who would hopefully arrive soon to rescue her.

Lucy strolled around the bend, exclaiming, "Oh, Sarita! What a blessed relief to see such a familiar!"

"Umm, I'm Sarah."

"Oh, of course you are," she wailed pitifully, stopping before Sarah who took just a few, tiny steps back.

"Oh, dear Sarah, hast thou seen my beloved Josh?"

"Uhh, are we talking about Josh White here? 'Cause if we are, umm, he's sort of taken, you know."

Lucy stared as though her entire world hinged upon the fact of Josh's devotion to her and as if Sarah just crushed that world mercilessly, before letting out such an unexpected, horrible howl that Sarah jumped.

"*Oh, has that Rachel stolen my Joshy-pu also with her womanish wiles?*" she sobbed.

"No, actually, he's lost to Krystal's wiles." Sarah placed an arm half-annoyedly, have-consolingly about the pitiful creature's trembling shoulders. "But do you know what I heard?"

"Nothing that could end my misery, I'm sure," she sniffed.

No, but it could sure end mine. "I overheard Nate Foot saying the other day how he dreamed of you as his 'leettle lemone drop.'"

The sobs ceased in an abrupt hiccup as she looked up with wide, hopeful eyes and tear-stained cheeks, breathing in a quivering voice, "Really? He called me 'leetle?'"

"Sure did."

"And a 'lemone drop?'"

"Yup."

She giggled girlishly before exclaiming, "Oh, dear Sasha—"

"Umm, Sarah—"

"I am forever in your debt, dear Sonya. I shall find him right now and profess my undying love!"

Sarah shook her head as Lucy frolicked off like a doting doe in search of her beloved, thinking to herself how she would, hopefully, later be able to laugh at this uncanny first date of hers. She was just thinking how she'd proved right all along—dating was nothing but yet another hazard to add to the long list of hazards in her life—when Mike strolled around the corner. All hazardous feelings melted away as he beamed at her, eyes glittering radiantly.

"Ready, my lady?" He offered his arm.

"Indeed, kind sir." She took his arm, holding it very close.

He led her into the pleasantly cool, night air and into the infamous school garden. The moon washed milky, dreamy waves of light across each petal and leaf, and it was this sight, coupled with Mike's warmth beside her and the fact that she really *was* on her first date—which truly *was* admittedly exciting—that sent excited shivers coursing through her. She whispered in such an elated, curious tone she thought she'd only ever hear from Chasmira, certainly not herself, "So, where exactly are we going, Mike?"

He only smiled his half-grin, which was in no way diminished in being only a *half*-grin, and his eyes twinkled playfully. "You'll see when we get there. You'll see...close your eyes."

"What?"

He sighed then jumped behind her and placed his hands over her eyes before she had a chance to blink.

She laughed. "How'd you do that?"

"Super-speed," he explained casually, "my special ability. You could call me a Superman wanna-be, I guess."

She chuckled again.

"Okay, now walk very carefully forward, and I'll steer you."

She walked forth, trusting, and he did not drive her into any trees or cause her to trip over any strange herbs. Though she was fairly certain that, at one point, she heard a distant, "Hooshy-wa!"

"You can stop now," he said at last.

She halted, he behind her.

"Here we are." He drew his hands away from her eyes.

She took in her breath, nearly squealing, forcing back the uncanny, high-pitched noise by thrusting a hand over her mouth. Surrounding her on all sides were roses, red ones, yellow ones, pink ones, white ones, strung in trees, bushes, their petals blanketing the ground like a royal carpet all her own.

"You like?"

She nodded, laughing lightly. "I love."

"I'm glad, especially as you'll have to spend a few moments here alone. I forgot our food."

They shared another chuckle as he slipped back into the trees.

Sarah sat on the plush quilt of grass and rose petals, gazing up and watching them flutter down about her like a gentle rain, when someone stumbled into the clearing, falling at her feet with a loud, "Umph!"

"There you are, my leetle lemone drop!"

She stared as he sat up, adjusting the infamous beret. She ogled as if the hat were an axe stuck through his skull or as if some other Halloween horror loomed before her. This could *not* be happening. She could *not* tolerate it. This was meant to be her first real, official date ever. She would *not* let it be interrupted a third time, for Pete's, or rather Mike's, sake.

"Hey, Nate," she said quickly. "Guess who I saw looking for you just a few moments ago?"

"Who?"

"Lucy."

"Lucy?" His brows raised, eyes glittering hopefully. "The gorgeous, intelligent, cheeky, leetle blonde creamseeckle?"

"Umm...sure..."

"Oh, how long 'ave I desaired to hear her blessed voice pine for me, and me alone! Forgive me, my leetle lemone drop, but our leetle affair must come to an end! My heart yearns for another."

"Yeah, sure, no offense taken."

"Oh, you are too kind. Deed you see vhich direction she vent?"

"Yeah, she was wandering about the school, looking for you."

"Oh, bless you, bless you! I vill never forget the time ve spent together, my leetle lemone drop!"

He raced stumbling from the clearing, laughing giddily as his shirt caught on a thorn, and then, moments later, he was gone.

Presently, Mike returned with a basket, sitting beside her and asking, "Was someone else here just now?"

"Nope."

"Swear I heard you talking to someone."

"Just talking to the flowers."

He laughed. "Get lonesome that quickly, did you?"

"Only for you." She sighed contentedly. She never thought she'd utter such cheesy but lovely words either. "Only for you..."

CHAPTER 8

"Heh, heh, so, umm, I know how in the past we've pranked each other like enemies almost, like, every time we go on a date, but this time I wanted to give you something I *know* you'll like—well, I don't *know* if you'll like it, but you'll at least appreciate its certain safety..."

Krystal studied him curiously as he dug around in his pocket and presented a crumpled piece of paper.

She arched a brow. "What? Trash from the dumpster? I think I preferred the risky gifts..."

"Not trash," he assured, unfurling the paper. "Well, that's yet to be determined, but...I wrote it a while ago, it's not much, but it's how I feel and stuff...

'Does she know how much I love her?

Does she know how much I care?

How my every thought is of her?

How I want to follow her everywhere?

Could I ever show her?

Could I ever dare?

Loyal friend, honest, true

Diligent in all you do

A blessing from Amiel above,

But most of all, Krystal, you are...love.'"

On that last word, he looked up with hopeful sincerity.

She took in a breath, struggling against the tears.

"Josh, that's the most beautiful thing you've ever...I..."

"I love you, Krystal."

She took in her breath again, more sharply this time, unable to tear from those glistening, sincerely blue eyes. She opened her mouth to reply when he

37

leaned in, kissing her, tenderly, yet it was not a short kiss. It stretched long and beautiful. Kissing her more deeply, his lips embraced hers with a more fervent passion, and he clutched her ardently to himself. His hands wove in her silky hair, like strands of gold woven from the purest sunlight...

Krystal suddenly thought to glance at her watch. Pulling away prematurely from the kiss, she cried, "Oh, shoot! I'll be right back." Springing up, she ran off, leaving Josh staring thoroughly confused, agitated, disappointed, wondering whether he should've bought those banana-peppermint-flavored breath mints after all.

It was 9:01. The fireworks exploding in her heart and within every pore of her skin made her late for Aaron's own fireworks. She hurried as fast as she could, in no way desiring to give Aaron something to mock her for later. She could just hear him... "I know you can't read, but I thought you could *at least* read a watch." She was scolding herself for agreeing to help him at all in the first place when she caught sight of Hailey and Sam and stopped short.

They stood beneath a tree, tapping on its trunk then putting their ears up to the bark as if listening intently for something. The remains of tofu lay scattered on the ground. It was certainly the strangest-looking date—or "outing," she reminded herself—that Krystal ever saw.

She stood staring until she suddenly remembered her mission and again glanced at her watch. 9:02. She made a mad dash towards the phoenix clearing.

* * *

Chasmira slowly opened her eyes. It was very dark and a bit chilly. Her head lay on something soft that gently and steadily rose and fell. As her eyes began to focus, she saw stars glittering above her, and everything rushed back to her—the wondrous dinner, the fireworks, especially the heart-shaped ones. How Aaron weaved her a crown from flowers and set it upon her head, along with the red phoenix feather she gave him long ago, the one he now wore on a golden chain about his neck. She smiled contentedly. She could still feel Aaron's arm around her and she snuggled closer against his chest, burrowing into the cuddly blue sweater. She was here. This was real. *He* was real. *They* were real.

Chasmira glanced at her glow-in-the-dark watch. The candles long since extinguished themselves, so the only light to see by was the stars. Pressing the watch's button, it read one o'clock in the morning, way past the school's curfew. She figured they may as well stay here and sneak back to campus in the morning. No need to wake Aaron. She was perfectly content enough to risk the trouble. She felt no desire to leave, and Aaron's calm, secure breathing signified he was fast asleep. Besides, Aaron could turn them both invisible, if need be, to sneak back the next day. Chasmira smiled contentedly as she laid her head back on his chest, snuggling just a little closer. She just closed her eyes again when she heard a noise.

The sound pulsed like the steady beat of a drum. Curious, Chasmira arose, careful not to disturb Aaron, quietly leaving the clearing in search of the sound. Soon she heard not only the steady beat but a mysteriously alluring tune playing on a flute. How drawn she was to it, so drawn she did not notice the jade-green bracelet glowing upon the arm hanging loosely like lead at her side. The captivating melody consumed her mind all the more the closer she approached its source. Her heart accelerated with the realization of the frighteningly overwhelming power the song held over her. Yet her conscious could not stop her feet from forcing her farther away from her unaware protector.

CHAPTER 9

"No, Chasmira, no, stay here..."

Still, she raced faster and faster towards the consuming cloud of darkness, real, true, literal darkness, a darkness from which he knew she could not return.

Fear drowned him. Helplessness consumed him. Courage failed him. He could only stand and scream.

"Chasmira!"

He bolted upright, sweating, panting, and thanking Amiel that it was just a terrible nightmare.

But it felt *so real*.

And it was not the first time he dreamt such a real and living nightmare.

He reached out to touch the grass beside him, feeling—

A nothingness. Only the grass itself, its soft comfort mocking him.

He jumped to his feet, stumbling from the clearing.

"Chasmira!"

Branches tore at his arms, his legs. He crashed into trees, tripping in his frantic search, but the consuming fear blocked out all presence of physical pain.

He raced through the garden, hysterically shouting Chasmira's name. He emerged from the garden, and a tall hill stretched up before him. Chasmira was nearly at the top, walking slowly towards some sort of dark portal, seemingly in a trance.

"Chasmira!" Aaron bounded up the hill towards her. For a moment, she paused.

"Chas—" Aaron tripped, falling hard to the ground. But the throbbing pain did not matter, *nothing* mattered save—

Chasmira continued on towards the portal.

Aaron scrambled up and raced towards her, reaching the top just in time to see her walk through the portal which snapped shut. The petals of her flower crown blew about him, broken, frail as something fluttered to the ground, landing at Aaron's feet. It was Chasmira's phoenix feather, the one he wore on a thin, gold chain about his neck. The one he wove in her hair only hours ago.

* * *

The spell's overpowering hold released her instantly upon her entering the portal, and she fell to the hard ground, body suddenly numb, being abruptly returned its freedom. Though the song's sway on her body did not last long, it had been intense.

She took in a sharp, gasping breath as the cold shocked her. Icy, rough surface beneath her. Chilling air sweeping through her struggling lungs which were themselves, still realizing their own independence once more. It was an effort to slide her eyelids up just enough to see dim light, something reddish but blurred in the small vision which her narrowed eyes allowed to penetrate. Gradually, though, the vision cleared, she was able to flex her eyes open and closed, blinking slowly as the numbness vanished from them completely.

As soon as the muffled laugh echoed softly in her ears, she recognized the stark silence surrounding her. The snicker also grew in its clarity as the seconds ticked past, and a different sort of iciness gripped her as she sensed a freeze within the chime-like voice.

She sat up, slowly, and then, looking up, gasped, scrambling backwards only to find herself pinned against the wall. A tall lady stood before her, skin fair and ghost-like. Her eyes and short, straight hair gleaming in the dim torch light with all the colors of the rainbow. Long, blood-red cloak spilling over her shoulders. Ebony staff clutched powerfully in one, slender hand, the end of it curving into a serpent's menacing head.

"Chasmira Eriz, we meet yet again," she cooed, smiling, eyes glinting cruelly. "Although, we have not yet really met formally, have we?"

"Who are you?" Chasmira breathed, wanting to speak louder, sound bolder, narrow her eyes in the same, threatening fashion as those Prismatic, icy spheres of the red-cloaked woman. But fear kept them open just enough for the dark lady to smirk coyly to herself.

"Hmm, yes...I *was* different then, so you wouldn't remember."

She tapped the end of her staff on the ground once. Instantly, a different woman stood before Chasmira, a girl of dark skin, dark hair, alluring, seductive eyes and smile, a revealing, silky, white dress, a familiar untrustworthy gleam in those tempting, onyx spheres...

As she changed back to her Prismatic form, Chasmira gasped, "Camille—Rorrim's servant."

"No. Camille, Rorrim's *faithful* sister," Camille hissed, her eyes narrowing just a little more, emanating just a bit more hatred.

Chasmira's eyes grew just a little wider. "His sister? But how, I—how can that be?"

"He sent me—and our *other* sister—away when he became king." Her head rose just a little bit more as his memory flashed like fire in those freezing eyes. "He recognized our great talents, our great potential, and so, for a time, he sent us away to a sect of private tutors, fairies skilled in all magics, including the dark arts. He also wanted to free us of the influence of that scum whom we were forced to acknowledge as our brother, Tobias.

"I returned to Rorrim when I heard how you and that filthy half-breed boyfriend of yours overthrew his reign. I failed him then in my attempts to lead you astray, to destroy you before you had another chance to destroy *him*. I failed him then, but I will *not* fail him now. Now, I shall harness one of the same, ancient powers he once sought after and use it to avenge him, bringing all Loz under the dominion of our family's name, just as he would have wanted..."

Her eyes wandered up, and Chasmira, trembling, followed her gaze, clasping her hand over her mouth as she took in another, staggering gasp. Strung along three of the shadowy stone walls encircling her hung three maidens, whom she imagined, by their yet faintly glowing billows of hair, their silks hung loosely upon their elegant figures, had once been very beautiful. Indeed, they were still lovely, but they shone now with an eerie, deathly pallor. Their chalky white forms and the dark recesses beneath their eyes gave the appearance of corpses strung upon the walls by the chains which held them there. Though Chasmira could see, or perhaps she just hoped in that dim light, their chests yet rising and falling with the feeble breath of life.

"I've been using my music to lure all of the secret sisters to me, slowly draining them of their power, although, of course, not all the way—they must all remain alive for me to be able to utilize the full powers of the bracelets themselves. But when I discovered that Julie, Eric's sister, did not wear her bracelet, that caused a bit of a problem..."

She turned her proud smile from the three fairies to Chasmira, triumphant eyes glittering darkly.

"But now, I've found *you*..."

Chasmira's horrified gaze lingered upon the suspended, limp forms of the fairies a moment more before she turned her eyes back to Camille and breathed,

"What do you plan on doing with me?"

Camille's eyes snapped to the glowing bracelet hanging upon Chasmira's wrist, that curse which dangled so freely yet which she could not be freed of. Chasmira took in a shallow breath. She knew precisely what Camille intended.

The other bracelet clung warmly to her wrist. Aaron. How she wished, now more than ever, for his comforting arms to drown her fear, for his love and assurance to set fire to the overwhelming fear she now suffered. He had always been her stability. She'd not felt so frightened with him by her side. But now that she was here, facing an eternal fate worse than death, with no hope of him finding her, it seemed...

No, she must cling to whatever frail hope she yet possessed and pray Amiel provide some way, would be able to let Aaron know where she was, how to reach her...

Camille smirked as she watched the tears slip down Chasmira's cheeks.

She held up one edge of her cloak of billowing, crimson shadow. As she dramatically whisked it aside, in her hand hovered a round, black, iridescently shimmering object. Shapes moved within it and all too quickly formed into a dreadfully familiar figure.

"Ahh, look into the crystal," Camille commanded slyly. "Look who approaches the hill. Is it not your beloved Aaron? I believe I shall open the portal and bring him to me. I have not yet had the chance to wreak revenge upon him for destroying my brother."

"Rorrim destroyed himself!" Chasmira shouted weakly.

"Silence, fool!" Camille waved her staff, throwing Chasmira against the cavern's wall. Chasmira's vision blurred. She felt for the bracelet—Aaron's—wanting her last memory to be of him, and yet, she did not feel it. After a moment of sorrowful panic, she became unconscious, unaware as a hideous creature slinked towards her helpless form.

CHAPTER 10

"Nathan! Josh! Rachel—!"

"Dude, like, what's going on?"

Josh, Krystal, Rachel, and Nathan surged into view from different directions, running beside him.

"Chasmira," he panted. "Gone...disappeared...portal..."

"What?" Rachel snapped. "You let her out of your sight?"

"We were sleeping. I didn't think—"

He stopped abruptly. That was just it. He didn't think of anything except of the joy of having her fall asleep in his arms, a joy he may never experience again because of his stupidity, his neglect...

"We'll find her," Sarah assured firmly as she joined them, holding Mike's hand as he ran alongside her.

Aaron paused in a clearing where Hailey and Sam bent over, observing a puke-green herb.

"Hooshy-wa! Do you have *any clue*—?"

"None of your herb-scolding right now, Hailey," Aaron snapped. "Chasmira —she's missing. And I had this awful dream..."

"Well, let's not panic." Rachel cast a dreading look at the others who knew Aaron's unfortunate history of darkly prophetic dreams.

"That's right." Nathan nodded. "Now, about this portal you were speaking of..."

"Right, it was on a hill, a—I can't remember now, there's so many stupid hills around this garden!" He held his head, everything swirling into a formless, panicked mass.

"It's okay!" said Nathan. "We'll all split up, look for it, meet in the phoenix clearing when we've found out how to get there."

Aaron nodded and they all rushed off in different directions.

Hot tears blinded Aaron as he ran almost aimlessly. Was it because he knew already in his heart that she was gone, a veil of invisible yet undeniable separation standing between them...?

He froze as he heard it. A melody. A calling, alluring, tempting, yet jeeringly beautiful melody...

He broke into a run again then jumped up, soaring towards the source of the ominous song...

As he emerged from the canopy of trees, before him rose a high, steadily sloping hill which he coursed up. The others soon emerged from all angles, rushing towards the music which echoed loudly until, abruptly, once they scaled halfway up the hill, it ceased.

"What, for the love of Pete, was that?" growled Sarah as they all joined Aaron. He stood panting, glaring at the nothingness which had, moments before, been an invisible yet clearly drawing force.

"They're taunting us," he breathed. "They know we're here..."

"Who?" asked Rachel shakily.

"Whoever's after the bracelet...whoever has Chasmira..."

A huge, black portal sprang open before them at the top of the hill, and they jumped back in surprise.

"That's it!" Aaron cried, jolting towards it.

"Stop!" Rachel grabbed his arm. "Don't you think it's a bit coincidental that the portal opens just as we're wanting it to?"

"Yeah, Rachel's right," agreed Nathan. "Something's fishy about all this."

"Guys, Chasmira's in trouble." Aaron eyed them each seriously, frustrated. Didn't they understand her safety was the most important thing in all the world?

"I *have* to help her. She's my best friend, and what's more, I love her."

Aaron headed towards the portal, and as they all started after him, he stopped and turned.

"And I'm going alone."

They all stared.

"*Are you insane?*" Sarah exclaimed.

"Well, actually he *is*," mumbled Krystal.

"Look, Nathan's right. Something's very wrong with this portal. I have a bad feeling. I don't want to drag you all into something dangerous. Stay here and wait for me. If something goes terribly wrong, go get Amanda Danielle. Chasmira left the stone in her room."

He took a step forward when Nathan held him back.

"Wait a sec, buddy."

He stretched forth his hand, brow furrowed in deep concentration as he muttered some magic beneath his breath.

Instants later, he clutched Aaron's sword in his hand.

"See." He handed it to his friend with a smirk. "I know how to do at least a little more than materialize food and summon computers."

"Thanks." Aaron clenched the hilt tightly in one hand.

He took a last, solemn look at each of them. Nathan placed his hand on Aaron's shoulder.

"We'll be praying for you—and for Chasmira."

Aaron nodded. As he entered the portal, it snapped shut behind him.

CHAPTER 11

Aaron was falling, falling through seemingly endless, blank time and space, just falling, falling, falling...

Thump. He landed against a hard surface. It took his eyes a little while to adjust to the dim light, but finally, some narrow, dark, stone passage was made clear. Light scintillated on the wall several feet down. *The light must radiate from an adjoining passage.*

Standing, he started down the passageway. As he reached the end and turned the corner, he found he was right. Torches lined the next corridor. They were black, carved in the form of serpents, and fire issued from their mouths.

He hurried down the eerie hall and gasped in horror upon entering the next chamber.

It was a huge room, and the ominous, serpent torches also hung all along the walls, casting an unfriendly, orange glow about the room, bouncing strange, dark shadows upon the walls, in the corners. But what horrified him most of all were the three young ladies chained to three of the walls. How fair they appeared, yet very pale, as though almost dead.

Walking up to one, he reached up to touch the hem of her dress. How familiar she looked with her long, silver hair, so much like his mother...

"Familiar, is she? Don't waste your time, though. She won't wake up."

Aaron wheeled at the sound of the woman's cool, emotionless voice. He stared. It was Camille, ex-servant of Rorrim, and she wore a long, blood-red cloak which stretched to the floor, its crimson river trailing behind her.

"Camille?" he breathed.

She laughed a quiet, uncomforting laugh as she transformed back into her Prismatic self.

"Surprised we meet again, ehh, Aaron? You shouldn't be, after what you did to my brother..."

Her eyes narrowed, blazing with a spite-ridden fire.

Aaron could only continue to stare as the reality of her words slowly dawned on him, too slowly for him to quite take it in. A surreal quality clung to the sudden revelation.

Finding his voice, glancing at the corpse-like ladies strung about the wall, crudely like party decorations, he uttered, "What have you done to them...and to Chasmira?"

"Hmm...that's quite an interesting tale. Have you ever heard of the Secret Sisters?"

Aaron slowly shook his head.

"Long ago, Zephyr gave to four sisters four magical bracelets said to hold great powers of rain, snow, wind, and fire. They were commanded to use these elemental bracelets to control these elemental powers, for those before them tried to abuse such powers. But if these powers could be contained within these bracelets, and if the keepers of the bracelets could become masters of these powers, they could defend Loz against any who might try to abuse the ancient elemental magics again.

"However, if they'd so chosen, they could have so easily used those powers to claim Loz for their own. Such is the foolishness of selflessness..."

"How can you say it's foolish?" Aaron sneered, his boldness returning as the incredulous reality began to sink into his mind. "How can you say it's foolish when you saw plainly where a lack of it led your brother?"

"My brother made many mistakes," Camille hissed icily, eyes darting at Aaron in a cold way that literally sent shivers throughout his entire body. "His greatest fault was his desire, however selfish, for the Daniels girl. In harming her life, he hesitated, though it may not have seemed obvious to you...

"But *I*." Her eyes flashed with a dangerous, already-victorious glint. "*I* won't make those same mistakes. I will pick up where my brother left off. I will avenge his death. And I will start here..."

Her eyes trailed greedily to the limp bodies of the ghost-like fairies.

"The fairies—Barbara, Julie, and Sylvia—will not wake up except at my command or my defeat, the latter concept not worth mentioning since I hold the fire bracelet, most powerful of the four. None of them alone possess the power to defeat me, nor are they in any such condition at this time.

"As for Chasmira, not only did I need Julie's bracelet from her, but I decided to use her as bait to lure you to me and thus obtain revenge for my brother,

Rorrim. While the fairies on the walls are only asleep, I prepared something special for your little friend..."

Camille flipped her cape aside to reveal Chasmira sprawled on the floor, pale and lifeless.

"She's fading fast. Indeed, she's almost gone. I'd come kiss her good-bye if I were you, Aaron Ruiz."

He didn't think twice, rushing towards Chasmira, sword clenched tightly as an incredible anger, passion, fury, desire flooded his every fiber, echoed within every recess of his heart. He jumped up, flying to pick up speed, he was mere inches from her—

Everything changed in an instant. In Camille's place loomed a huge, blood-red serpent. Her tail snapped forth like a whip, thrusting him back with little effort. Stunned, he catapulted nearly to the far wall, skidding hard across the floor.

He lay dazed for a moment, but as his vision cleared, he saw her cruel fangs and white, empty eyes towering over, leering at him. Sensation returned to his momentarily numb body. Realizing the sword miraculously still clasped in his hand, he held it tight, rolling aside as she struck with lightning speed and incredible accuracy.

The next few moments were nothing but a blur as he slipped in and out of her coils, nicking her tough skin here and there with the blade, causing her to hiss defiantly. But she moved too swiftly and skillfully for him to get in any good hits. He needed some sort of strategy...

At some point—he didn't know when, for he was too busy weaving and dodging—she surrounded them, himself, herself, Chasmira, with a ring of flame that reduced the room he had to maneuver, shrunk the fighting rink, shrunk his chances...

A sharp pain surged through his arm, intensifying with each quarter of a second 'til he felt first ice, then fire, then a tearing, clawing sensation, then all three pains merging together into one, nearly maddening effect. He stumbled, wanting to clutch at that arm, claw the pain away, but the slightest touch made him shout in agony all the more.

Gradually, his arm began to grow numb, the pain to lessen, though his body felt its strength steadily draining. He still held the sword firm, nearly falling over as he struggled to stand straight, get his bearings, find Camille, find Chasmira...

Camille whipped her tail in the air once more, knocking Aaron to the ground. His body ached all over now. He grimaced as he hit hard against the cavern's floor. His vision was beginning to blur, his senses to weaken, both from the poison of Camille's wound and the stifling heat and smoke from the fire.

He felt so weak, so tired. Yet as he glanced over and saw Chasmira's frail form, her ghostly white skin, her shallow breathing, he knew she yet fought to stay alive with her last bit of strength. He knew he must fight as well, for her sake.

With Camille's last blow, his sword was knocked from his hand. It lay only a few inches from his fingertips. He stretched out his hand until he felt his fingers closing around the hilt. A shadow passed over him as the serpent towered over him, her crimson scales glinting in the glow of the flames.

Camille lunged towards him with her cruel, white dagger-teeth, but he hefted the sword and drove it into her.

It was the only blow needed, and the three other sisters—Barbara, Julie, and Sylvia—awoke with the instant weakening of Camille's power, their chains shattering, releasing them from their imprisonment. They flew from the walls and hovered over Aaron. Together, they combined their powers until the crystal blade glowed brighter than Aaron ever saw it glow before.

"Now," cried Julie. "Deliver the final blow!"

Aaron felt a new strength surge through him as he struggled to his feet and brought the sword crashing down on his foe.

Camille gave a final, horrifying screech before vanishing forever.

The cavern shook violently as great chunks of burning rock crashed down from the ceiling.

"We must go before the entire thing collapses!" Barbara shouted over the tumult, spreading her hands as if ripping an opening in the air itself; a portal opened before them.

Aaron rushed over to Chasmira. How weak she appeared, barely clinging to life. How light she felt as Aaron picked her up and carried her through the portal, the fairies hurrying after him.

CHAPTER 12

Rachel paced across the crest of the hill impatiently.

"It's been *forever*. They should be back by now! What if something horrible —"

"Should we get Amanda—?" Nathan began.

A bright light suddenly shone all about them as a portal opened atop the hill, pure white emanating from within.

From the portal stepped Aaron, his clothes torn, dirty, and blood-stained, his face weary, yet his expression unwavering, resolute to get Chasmira to safety. He carried her frail, unconscious form in his arms, as behind him followed three fairies, beautiful and magnificent to behold.

Rachel immediately recognized Barbara as her sister, and catching each other's eye, they shared a brief smile before becoming grave. Rachel turned her concern towards Aaron and Chasmira, she and the others rushing to them as Aaron gently laid Chasmira on the soft grass and knelt down beside her.

"Aaron, will she be alright?" Sarah asked, pale with fear.

Aaron looked up hopefully at the three fairies. All wore grave faces, and tears sparkled in Sylvia's eyes as she saw her brother's pain. Julie too was on the verge of tears so Barbara replied, "She's been poisoned by Camille's venom, and I'm afraid the only cure is a phoenix feather, but they're very rare—"

Aaron removed the feather from the gold chain around his neck and handed it to the great fairy who at first looked at him in surprise. Then she set to work, rubbing it in her hands until it turned into a gold and red, glittering powder. This she sprinkled over Chasmira's limp body.

They all held their breath, waiting, praying fervently. Slowly, her eyes opened. Chasmira smiled faintly as she found herself gazing up at Aaron.

He smiled back. "How do you feel?"

"Tired, but better," she answered quietly, then frowned. "But *you...you* look awful..."

Everyone suddenly noticed the dark circles beneath his eyes, his blanched skin. Aaron could feel his breathing growing more difficult again. The poison yet gripped him.

Sylvia caught a glimpse of the wound in his arm where Camille sunk her fangs. It loomed black and grotesque.

"Aaron, your arm." Sylvia's eyes stared gravely. "Why didn't you tell us?"

"Aaron, what's going on?" asked Chasmira. "Are you okay?"

"Yeah, I—I'm fine," he began, but his vision blurred again. Everything blackened.

* * *

Sylvia sat on the edge of Aaron's bed, gently stroking his soft, ebony hair.

"I'm just glad I finally got to see you again...know that you're alright..." he breathed.

She smiled weakly.

"Chasmira," he continued, "she doesn't know I used the phoenix feather to save her life instead of mine, does she?"

"No."

"Good. It's better she doesn't know. I know how guilty she'd feel if she—"

Outside the room, they could hear Chasmira crying, nearly shrieking, "*What do you mean you can't do anything? There must be something, anything, try everything—!*"

"Chasmira, I'm so sorry." Julie tenderly placed a hand on her shoulder. "But the only cure is a phoenix feather, and they are so rare—"

"But he *has* one! I *gave* it to him! He always wears it around his neck—"

"He is too far gone." Sylvia stepped from the room. Julie cast her a grateful look. Of course, this was not true, but Aaron instructed all of them not to tell Chasmira the full truth of the horrors which occurred that night.

Chasmira tried very hard not to cry as her eyes flashed desperately to each of their faces, with a deeper, realer pain than any of them had ever seen. *Aaron can't die.* Not only was he one of her closest friends, but he was the first and only guy she ever really, truly loved, and she'd finally been able to express her love to him. She finally began to hope in the fact they might someday be together forever, just as she dreamed for so long, for she knew within her heart he began to love her too. He couldn't just leave her now, now that she finally dared to open up her heart to that hope. He couldn't really be dying, could he...?

"He wants to see you," Sylvia managed finally, choking back a sob as she saw the pain and torment etched on Chasmira's face.

Chasmira nodded. She took a deep breath, trying to compose herself for his sake alone, then opened the door and walked through.

However, as soon as she saw the light from the fireplace shining upon his pale form, all composure left her, and she could no longer hold back the tears. He looked so frail. His breathing was so unsteady and came in short, rasping breaths. How quickly he faded. His once happy, care-free expression and strong form were now so weak, so fragile. She knelt beside him and laid her head on the bed, weeping uncontrollably.

Aaron weakly lifted his hand and stroked Chasmira's thick, golden waves. She never looked so angelically beautiful and yet so sad and tragically pitiful all at once. How he longed to comfort her, but nothing he could say would ease her pain and sorrow.

"Don't cry," he said softly. "I don't like to see you cry...I always loved your smile, you know..."

Chasmira lifted her tear-streaked face and managed a small smile.

Aaron returned the grin. "That's better...now, look on the table..."

Chasmira glanced at the table beside his bed and gasped. There lay the bracelet Aaron gave her.

"Found among the ruins of the cavern," Aaron managed. It was growing harder for him to talk as his breathing grew more difficult.

She slipped it on her wrist and barely whispered, "I'll wear it and remember you every day..." She wanted to tell him how much she loved him and would miss him, yet her sobs overcame, choking down the words.

But he could read the message in her eyes, and gently brushing a tear from her cheek, caressing her face, he breathed softy, "I love you too, Cassy..."

Then his eyelids slowly closed. She gasped, inching closer as if the pleading gaze of her own eyes could will his to linger open just a little longer. Chasmira took his hand. So cold. She laid her head on the bed again and wept.

* * *

"The Lord is my Shepherd. I shall not want..."

53

Chasmira's mind wandered from Pastyre Saltzgiver's reading of the twenty-third Psalm. She gazed up at the lofty trees as the wind gently rustled them. They were beginning to change colors as fall approached, carried on the cold breeze of approaching winter.

Everyone gathered in the phoenix clearing where Aaron wished to be buried. Here, in their special place, a place which once served as a shrine of comfort and friendship, now a reminder of death and sorrow...

"He leadeth me beside the still waters..."

The events of that dreadful night flashed through Chasmira's mind. Though no one told her about the phoenix feather, somehow she knew in her heart he used it to save her life. She'd been poisoned as well. Where else would they have gotten one from?

She recalled also her conversation with Julie that morning...

Chasmira sat in the phoenix clearing, crying softly. She heard a rustle in the bushes and looked up to see Julie approaching. She sat down next to Chasmira, taking her hand.

"Chasmira, I'm so sorry about Aaron..."

"Thank you," Chasmira replied softly, all spirit vanished from her eyes. Julie nearly cried too.

"I feel somewhat responsible for his death."

Chasmira stared.

"Well," continued the fairy. "If Eric never gave you that bracelet of mine —"

"Oh, no," Chasmira reassured. "Eric couldn't have known. It's neither your fault nor his, and I don't blame you at all."

"Thank you," Julie sighed.

Chasmira sighed as well. "Of course. Besides, I have seen enough pain already. I would not cause you pain as well by blaming you for Aaron's death. What's done is done, and we must accept it as Amiel's will though we do not know yet what purpose He has in it..."

It was Julie's turn to stare. Her brother had been right. Chasmira was a wise, young, Amielian lady. Though she could tell how sorrowful Chasmira was over Aaron's death, she did not blame or hate anyone for it. Most of all, she did not lose her faith in Amiel, trusting that Aaron's death was a part of His will...

"Thy rod and thy staff, they comfort me..."

Chasmira remembered something Amanda Danielle said as she glanced up at the fairy who mourned beside her husband and two children weeping for their Uncle Aary, "Remember that Amiel understands what it feels like to be lonely. I know you feel as though no one understands what you're going through right now, but Amiel does. Take comfort in the fact He is always there to comfort you..."

"Surely goodness and mercy shall follow me all the days of my life, and I will dwell in the house of the Lord forever..."

Suddenly, a soft, sad song was carried on the air. It gradually grew clearer and louder, and they looked up in the sky to see four phoenixes approaching. Immediately, Chasmira knew them, the mother phoenix from whence Aaron's feather came and her children who once lived in the nest in the clearing.

They glided over the clearing, singing their sorrowful melody, and from the sky, tiny, shimmering spheres began to fall. The phoenixes were crying, their tears forming into pearls as they rained down.

Chasmira reached out to catch one of the pearls. As she held it in her hand though, she stared at it curiously. Unlike the other pearls falling around her, it was green. How rare green phoenix pearls were. She remembered learning about them in Science class. Mrs. White said they were a sign of new life and hope.

Something else fluttered from the sky and rested in her hand beside the pearl. It was a golden feather.

Chasmira and the others watched as the phoenixes soared off into the distance. Chasmira was not quite as sad though. She carefully pocketed the feather and pearl. Something was about to happen, she could feel it. They were indeed a sign of new hope.

* * *

Chasmira sat in the phoenix clearing, beneath the phoenix tree. She stared at the white, glistening tomb stone. Sylvia had planted moon blossoms all about it.

The three fairies walked into the clearing, and Chasmira arose to face them.

"We must leave now for a time," announced Barbara. "We have bid everyone else good bye and wanted to see you and thank you for all you've done."

Tears again came to Chasmira's eyes, and Barbara hugged her tenderly, whispering into her ear words of comfort.

Each of the fairies did the same, and when Chasmira finally came to Julie, she gazed deeply into her eyes. They were so blue, just like Eric's.

"Chasmira, it pains me to see you so sad."

"Sometimes I feel as though I shall never be happy again. Sometimes all I do is think about Aaron and cry."

"It will take time, much time. But, yes, you will find your joy again. Remember to trust Amiel to comfort you, for He will help you find that joy again. Trust in your friends as well, for they will want to comfort you also. You must comfort each other. And do not remember Aaron only as you last saw him and dwell on that day. Remember him as he was, full of life and full of love. Remember He is with the Lord Amiel, and you will see him again someday in Heaven. And...remember the phoenix feather."

Chasmira nodded then watched as the three fairies rose up into the sky and disappeared from view.

Someone else called her name. Rachel. She, Sarah, Krystal, and Hailey all stepped into the clearing.

"Hey, you okay?" Rachel placed an arm around Chasmira's shoulder.

"Yes." Chasmira smiled faintly, though her heart felt stifled and she wished she could feel nothing at all. "I'll be fine."

INTERLUDE

Soft grass tickled the bit of exposed, creamy skin. She hardly noticed this sensation, nor did she take much notice of the gentle breeze stirring about him save when it rippled through the thick waves of his hair, making each strand dance like a sunbeam woven of pure gold. No feeling existed except the flow of his velvety skin beneath her fingertips as they caressed his face. His calm breathing, steadily intensifying as her fingers skipped ever so lightly upon every crevice of his face, strong arms, chest. She dug her hands deep into his hair, thrilling as her flesh swam through the feathery waves, heart leaping sporadically as his own, strong hands pulled her closer. His lips embraced hers fervently, and she shivered as his body held hers captive in a strange but alluring combination of power and gentleness.

Breaking from yet another glorious kiss, she laid her head on his chest. As she stirred her fingers playfully across his skin, she allowed the tears to flow, fresh tears hidden too long behind the walls of necessary courage and strength. But now that she no longer needed to be his shelter, she needed him to be just that for her. So she hugged him close, tight as if he might vanish any moment like a frail dream. Burying her face against his warm flesh, she let the unstoppable tears cascade over his diamond body...

"Shh..." He stroked her hair in the tender way she so loved, holding her closer. "I hate this, hate to see you cry...I hate what she tried to do to us, my aunt, what she tried to take away. She tried to take away *this*—*us*. Doesn't she know how wrong that is...?"

Choking back a sob, she whispered, "Dristann, I know I was so strong for you then because I had to be. But I was really so scared. So scared that I wouldn't be able to get you out of there, pry you from her grasp. I've never been so scared...and now, I'm so terrified of losing you again..."

"But you won't. We are one now—no one can separate us. You said yourself that in being married, we are safe. Besides, I wouldn't have it any other way. Though...I wonder what would've happened if you didn't save me...?"

"I don't know...That's just it. The books...they never say...not knowing, that terrified me even more because I didn't really know how to help you. I had to use five of my ten wishes to find you, I was so afraid of running out, and then what...?"

"But you didn't." His embrace tightened more fervently. Awe trickled into his voice, intensifying with each passing word he uttered. "You got me out. You alone. There was no one else, no one who cared. But you loved me, *you* did that, *you*. You helped Aaron and Chasmira out of so many binds without their realizing, yet the one thing that most terrified you was really...losing me...There is

nothing you could do more to prove your love for me. I haven't figured out *why*
—" he smirked wryly— "but you truly do love me, that much is so clear to
me...and I love you too..."

Snuggling deeper into the niche between his arm and chest—how perfectly
their bodies fit, like two puzzle pieces designed to hug each other with tight pre-
cision—she glanced up at the tree house shadowing them. Between the thick
branches, stars glistened gaily. It was the most beautiful nook, situated just behind the tree house, in a private little hollow at the base of a gently sloping hill.

"It truly was kind of your friend to allow us to stay here," he mused.

"Mmm...well, he so loves visitors, and this is one of my favorite places besides, from one of my favorite stories. This tree house...He's like my brother,
you know? So many memories..."

"You've really seen a lot of places and helped a lot of people." Awe tinged
his voice again.

Her slender shoulders brushed against him as she shrugged. "That's what
story-travelers do...We travel into stories and help people. And now you get to
travel with me, help them too."

"That might do me well...accompanying my lovely, new wife on her min-
istry, saving others as she has saved me..."

"It wasn't me, really...Amiel saved you, I could not have done it without
drawing strength from my faith in him..."

"Mmm...Still, I think it was your faith which saved me. And I love you for it
so much, my love..."

"I love you too..."

They both jumped as a cow mooed loudly overhead.

He chuckled lightly. "Ever figure out how he got that thing up in the tree
house?"

She shrugged. "Some parts of the story you never do find out."

"Hmm, well, I know that whatever happens, the ending of our story, at least,
will be a good one."

She cuddled yet closer, eyes fast growing heavy. Inwardly praying it might
be so—there was still a long part of the story to go—she thanked Amiel as she
drifted to sleep, for the first time ever in her husband's arms.

THE SILVER KNIGHT

"Weeping may endure for a night, but joy cometh in the morning."
~ Psalms 30:5

"Hope is not the absence of sorrow, but the presence of God."
~ Christine E. Schulze

THE SECRET SISTER AND THE SILVER KNIGHT

CHAPTER 1

"Chasmira...Chasmira..." Rachel chanted softly, while Hailey added, "Yoo-hoo! Anyone home?"

The distant sadness lingered in her unresponsive gaze.

"Chasmira!" Rachel snapped more sharply. "Can I *please* borrow your English notes?"

"Mmm...sure..." Chasmira pushed the stack of notes over to Rachel absent-mindedly while Rachel, Sarah, Hailey, and Krystal all cast each deeply concerned looks.

Chasmira remained this way since Aaron's death. The hope she clung to at the first extinguished as the reality of each, slowly passing, lonely day dragged on. It was now December, so three months had passed. Yet, it seemed like only three days to her as she wandered the halls like a ghost, saying little, eating less, crying much. Some days she would sit and stare for endless hours at his grave, caressing a golden-red feather and a smooth, green pearl which she seemed to carry ever and anon in her pocket, or else twirling the diamond-studded bracelet upon her now even tinier wrist.

"Hey, look!" Krystal shouted. "It's Eric!"

Chasmira looked up. Indeed, Eric just entered the dining hall. He was still tall, handsome, and smiling, just as she last observed him. Yet as he spotted her and waved, she realized he was the last person she wanted to see right now. The tears snatched with their cruel fingers, threatening to tear her apart. Feebly, yet determinedly, she fought them back.

Eric soon joined them at their table, grabbing some bacon and eggs.

Josh eyed him slyly. "So, Eric, you've finally returned from your 'secret mission,' ehh?"

"Yep. And don't try getting details about it out of me like you always do."

Josh crossed his arms and scowled.

"So, how have you all been?" Eric asked.

They all voiced they were good, well, fine, or something of that nature, except Hailey who declared she would have to get back to him on that one. Nate and Lucy, who joined their table—after they got together with each other, both Josh and Sarah considered them redeemed, and they were so often absorbed in each other so as not to be particularly annoying to any other parties present— introduced themselves and Eric cast a playful twinkle at Sarah who merely rolled her eyes, admitting that, yes, she knew they were more than odd. Yet, despite the interest of old and new friends, Eric's attention drew primarily to Chasmira. She seemed even more beautiful than when he left but was so quiet and reserved, her expression blank, phantom-like, her skin pale, thin, drawn, shadows stirring darkly beneath her once glistening, blue eyes.

"So. How are you doing?"

Sarah gave him a look that said he better shut up or she would knock him in the head. Rachel proceeded to hit herself over the head with a notebook while Chasmira bit her lip as she continued to stare straight ahead, feeling the tears quickly winning their side of the battle and hating them for it.

Eric remained oblivious to any of this as he glanced about curiously. "And where is Aaron? I don't see him anywhere—"

A loud thud sounded as Chasmira's chair clattered to the floor. She shot up from her seat, racing, stumbling as she fled the dining hall.

"Oh, that was just peachy," Sarah snapped at Eric.

"Yeah, thanks a lot." Rachel rushed after Chasmira.

"What did I do?" Eric frowned, thoroughly confused.

"Eric, some things happened while you were gone..." announced Nathan gravely.

* * *

Chasmira ran as fast as she could to the garden, collapsing beneath the phoenix tree and sobbing bitterly, trying to allow the air to fill her lungs, struggling so desperately to breathe, to at least be able to feel that one, simple, normal sensation.

When she achieved this small victory at last, she crept over and knelt before the sparkling, white gravestone. White moon blossoms grew up to embrace it. She sat crying softly when Rachel's voice drifted from behind her, "Hey, thought I'd find you here."

Rachel walked over, knelt beside her friend, and placed an arm around her.

"Eric didn't mean anything. He just got back this morning. He didn't know."

"Chasmira?"

Eric knelt on the other side of Chasmira and placed a hand on her shoulder.

"Cassy—"

"Please don't call me that," she snapped, growing rigid at his touch.

Eric turned red yet persisted, "Chasmira. I'm so sorry. I didn't know. I didn't mean to hurt you."

"I know," she replied quietly.

A grave silence settled over them all before Rachel asked, "You coming back to breakfast?"

"I'd like a little more time...alone."

Eric glanced at Rachel who nodded, and together they rose and left the clearing. But Eric paused to peer through the trees at Chasmira, brow furrowed, eyes set tensely with concern, the familiar vein protruding from his forehead as he focused so fiercely.

"Eric?"

He sighed. "It pains me to see her this way. When I left, she was always so...cheerful...full of spirit and life. Now...she's all but dead, just existing."

"Yeah, I know."

"Rachel, can—can I tell you something?"

"Sure."

Eric motioned her to come closer, and he continued in a voice soft and low. "Before I left the school last time, I fell in love with Chasmira. I love her still, and I have every day since. I know she's just lost Aaron and misses him deeply, but maybe it would help her to know someone cares about her. What can I do to help?"

"Wow. Umm..." In part, she felt shocked. The whole school practically knew Eric liked Chasmira, but she was surprised and a little bit agitated he would even consider just declaring his feelings when he saw how utterly distraught she was by Aaron's loss. Still, perhaps someone to cling to was truly what she needed right now.

Finally, Rachel said, "Well, for now, just be there for her—be her friend. Comfort her and show her you care. But be understanding and patient. Remember that these things take time, and for Chasmira, it may take a lot more time than it takes most."

Eric nodded slowly, finally drawing his gaze away from Chasmira.

"Thanks." He followed Rachel back to the college. She did not reply, too busy wondering, hoping, praying she just granted the right advice.

CHAPTER 2

"Hey, Cassy."

"Mmm," she sighed.

"So, umm." Rachel half ignored, half wondered if she should heed the possible warning exploding in her head. Chasmira was looking at her, waiting. Rachel actually caught her attention. She *had* to decide something...

"Umm, me and Nate and a friend of ours are having a special dinner tonight in the dining hall. You know, Nathan's materializing our own food and whatnot, much better than dining hall food even. What do you say?"

Rachel noted the glitter in her eye. A quickly fading glitter, yes, but still, it flickered there. She made a pitiful attempt to smile. "Sure. I think I'd like that."

"Okay then," Rachel grinned in turn. "See you there at the normal time. Actually, I'll just pick you up, take you with me."

"You're sure I won't be infringing upon you and Nathan's time together?"

"No, no, not at all. See you then, okay, Cassy?"

"Okay."

* * *

Chasmira continued to lay on her back, staring at the ceiling, wondering what she committed herself to. Of course, she knew Rachel just tried to help, and perhaps a bit of fun would do her good. But perhaps it wouldn't. This wasn't the first time her friends, especially Sarah, tried to perk her up by supplying her with activities and other distractions, and while she knew they meant well, such supposedly happy times did naught save to make her feel even more sorrowful. They were times of joy that could not be spent with Aaron but which would have been if he were still here. She would always imagine, always picture in her head everything he might say or do or think was he there beside her, and sometimes she would get so immersed in such flights of fancy that she almost *did* feel happy again. But they were just that. Flights. And as soon as they took wing, the harsh reality plummeted down upon her even more starkly than before...

Chasmira sat up, fighting back the tears she was so weary of. She must try to focus on having a good time tonight. Would he not have wanted that? Of course he would. What was wrong with her? Sometimes she wondered if she did not really want to be happy again without him, did not really care to try. But she knew she must, for his own sake. He would have wanted it himself.

Dragging herself from the bed, she set her mind about getting ready. She knew she had to focus on that one thing—getting ready—lest the sorrows drown out all hope of thinking upon anything but the sorrow itself.

She searched her wardrobe for something sufficient. Her fuzzy sweater with the snowflakes, the one that curved elegantly about the soft curves of her body, as well as her dark blue jeans which also accented her small but lovely form. She curled her hair 'til it fell in a shower of ringlets about her face, and she even added a bit of makeup, which she hardly ever did because to her it was a waste of time, both because of her personal standards and by the mere fact she was a Scintillate and thus bore a natural glow. But applying the makeup and applying it slowly kept her focused, so she primped and fussed over herself for three whole hours until she heard the rapid rap. Giving a final fluff to a stray curl, she walked over and opened the door.

"Hey, Cassy—"

Rachel gaped, nearly tripping over the doorframe into the room.

"Umm...wow?"

"Wow what?" Chasmira asked in her now familiar yet still eerily distant, quiet voice.

"Wow...*you*. Man, what are you trying to do, make Nathan jealous or something?"

Chasmira smiled frailly. Even the smile's frailty was hauntingly beautiful. "I'm sure that wouldn't be possible. Nathan's so into you he still can't hardly form a coherent sentence around you sometimes."

"Yeah, that's true enough." Rachel rolled her eyes. "Well, let's get going then."

Chasmira stepped out and closed the door behind them.

As they slipped down the various corridors towards the dining hall, everyone stared, gaped, whispered. She did not notice but merely walked amongst them as some enchanting siren, some ghost-like figure of alluring prettiness. Her fair skin and vacant, staring eyes gave her that otherworldly look, yet they only intensified her charm all the more as she glided past.

As they graced the dining hall, passing through the crowds of students, an uncanny hush fell across all. The whispers finally culminated into their normal volume of talking again, but eyes strayed to her all throughout that evening, the impossibly gorgeous ghost-girl.

But there was one whose eyes stayed locked upon her from the moment she entered 'til the time she left. Chasmira saw him too as they approached the table from which Nathan waved them over, and she stared, horrified, the tears springing into her eyes once more. She trembled, fighting, forcing them back. Taking a deep breath, she held her head a little higher. She *had* to do this. Be normal. For Aaron's sake.

CHAPTER 3

A rare, precious, angelic, fragile creature. An angel of death and sorrow. A ghost returned from her grave, wandering the earth, vainly seeking consolation. An enchanting, broken woman, her heart still a girl's, crushed, in need of mending, in need of someone holding the pieces in their hand and weaving them back together. A beautiful girl whom he loved ever since he met her and could not keep his eyes off of, though he noted her uncomfortableness.

"Good evening, Chasmira." He rose, smiling, holding out her chair.

"Thank you, Eric," she said quietly, sitting, he across from her, though hesitatingly. She refused to look at him. Should he sit beside her where she would not constantly see his eyes boring into her beauty? Yet, if he sat to the side, she would still *feel* them, even if she looked away. So he remained seated as Rachel sat across from Nathan who flushed red, typing frantically on his laptop. She chirped cheerily, "Hullo, Nathan."

"Umm...hi, Rachel..."

"You know, this isn't an official date, you can calm down," Eric whispered to him.

"Umm...hi, Rachel..."

Rachel sighed, rolling her eyes for what Eric was certain would not be the last time that evening.

He turned to Chasmira, whose vacant stare focused on a spider crawling slowly up the far wall. "You look exceptionally lovely tonight, Chasmira."

"Thank you," she breathed emptily.

Rachel glanced at them, then at Nathan expectantly. She stared until he glanced up at her, smiled nervously for a half second, and then began banging yet more furiously upon the poor keys of his laptop.

"Nathan. We *are* here to eat and talk and stuff. Could you please—?"

"Oh, oh, yes, of course." He slammed the computer shut without an attempt to save any of his work—no doubt he would retype it on a later date with Rachel—and presenting a picnic basket from beneath the table, announced, "Everyone like chicken?"

Eric beamed. "I do. And I know Chasmira here does too. One of your favorites, isn't it?"

She nodded, trying to smile at him.

Nathan passed out the plates and napkins and proceeded to dole out the food 'til he spilled gravy all over Rachel's lap. She volunteered to pass out the food herself, rolling her eyes several times as he muttered frantically over and over just how truly sorry he was to be such a clumsy oaf.

The food arrangements settled and the prayers offered, they started the meal. Nathan seemed to focus very hard on eating his chicken. Chasmira ate hers uncommonly daintily, in Eric's opinion. Rachel attacked hers with a vengeance, glaring at Nathan very threateningly as Eric remarked upon the quality of the food then asked Chasmira how she liked it. Chasmira agreed she liked it very much indeed and he even caught a hint of a sparkle in her eyes as she smiled in a small yet not insignificant way at him.

"So, Chasmira." Eric smirked encouragingly at her, wanting nothing more than for her angelic glow to grow just a little bit brighter. "I hear that you've joined the college's choir?"

"Hmm? Oh, yes, I have." The sparkle intensified ever so slightly in her eyes. Eric's heart leaped, for he obviously hit the right chord in her heart.

"I didn't know you like to sing."

"I love it. Choir's the one thing that makes me believe I can be happy again some day...Ms. Chrysillee and everyone in the class are all so kind...It's like having a second family. And when I sing, I can release everything I'm feeling, whether the song is happy or sad. I love it."

"I'm glad." His eyes twinkled reassuringly. "You deserve something that can help you feel that way."

He glanced over at Rachel who glared at them a bit nastily. Then, she quickly turned away. Eric's eye then fell upon Sarah who sat several tables away, staring at them curiously 'til Mike tugged on her sweater, and she turned back around.

"So, umm, Nathan, what kind of computer program you working on today?" Rachel asked.

"Oh, umm, you know, normal stuff..." As if her words served as a prompt, he set down his fork upon the uncleared plate of food, drew the computer to him once more, and began ramming away on the poor keys.

Eye-roll number six. Eric stifled a laugh.

"So, what have you been up to, Eric?"

He started at the question, and then beamed. Chasmira didn't just speak but actually took the initiative to ask him something, show an interest in the conversation.

"Well, as Josh will tell you, I've been on a good deal of 'secret missions.' And I'm afraid they truly *are* secret, so I can't tell you anything about them. But I can say they involve a good deal of travel."

"How exciting." Her eyes gleamed just a bit more. "I always wanted to travel."

"Someday, you will." His gaze again reassured, and she looked down. At last, a healthy flush lighted softly upon her white cheeks.

The rest of dinner continued that way. He was able to make polite bits of conversation, safe conversation that did not upset her, and it seemed his gentleness and understanding helped her open up a bit. He continued to count Rachel's eye-rolls 'til they surpassed twenty-six, and by that time, supper was over and done with.

They departed with Eric offering to walk Chasmira to her room, announcing they really must all get together again sometime, to which Rachel nudged Nathan.

"Ehh, Nathan?"

"Umm...umm..."

This gained Eric his twenty-eighth eye-roll.

As Eric and Chasmira stopped before the door of her dorm room, he smiled down at her. "I had a good time with you tonight—and Rachel and Nathan, of course."

"I think...I did too."

She smiled a small but real smile, and he returned with a larger and most definitely real grin.

"I'll see you tomorrow?"

"Sure."

"Good night, Chasmira."

"Good night, Eric. Thank you."

She slipped into her room.

He stared at the closed door, that veil that stood between them 'til their next meeting, thinking how very welcome she was before he turned and walked slowly back to his own dormitory.

CHAPTER 4

Sarah watched them closely. It was their sixth dinner together, Eric, Chasmira, Nathan, and Rachel. Things only grew more sour between Nathan and Rachel to the point that Nathan only sat, ate, and typed, though much more quietly, routinely even, whilst Eric and Chasmira talked more and more, Chasmira smiled more, even laughed once—

"Sarah, love, you're doing it again." As Mike tapped her, she instinctively turned back to her unusually untouched chocolate pie.

"I really don't see what's so fascinating," Hailey mumbled. Sarah glared at her annoyingly. Of course, Hailey was repelled by anything that might seem in the slightest romantic.

"I think it's fascinating," Krystal sighed. "And it's good for Chasmira to have an interest."

"He's not an *interest*, he's, like, a friend," Josh reminded her. "I don't know if she's quite ready for an 'interest' yet."

Krystal stared. "There's a rare, possible word of wisdom spewing from your mouth."

He drew himself up proudly. "Heh, heh, I *do* have the wonderful ability to awe like that from time to time."

Sarah rolled her eyes then returned to her staring.

"Sarah, love..."

"I know, I know, it's just...I'm concerned. I don't think *Eric* thinks of *her* as less than an interest..."

"I think you're right too," agreed Lucy, as Nate snuggled her close and cooed, "Oh, my leetle lemone drop, how obsairvant you are..."

"Eric's a nice guy," Krystal said. "I think he likes her too, but I think he knows his boundaries..."

Sarah shook her head. "It's not just that. I think Rachel's having a problem with 'interest' herself..."

Their eyes followed her gaze to a past-disgruntled Rachel, who glared at the two as Eric said something and Chasmira laughed. Suddenly, she burst from her chair, yelling something that made Chasmira stare guiltily and Eric stare angrily as he found all his efforts dashed in one, fell swoop.

Rachel stormed from the dining hall, and Chasmira rose to pursue her when Eric placed a hand on her arm, trying to hold her back. She tore gently away, murmuring something with a yet more upset look in her eye, racing from the room in hopes to catch up with Rachel.

Sarah glanced uneasily at Krystal, Josh, and Mike who all returned the look, Hailey and Sam were poring over a book on North-western United States herbal remedies and were thus oblivious to the scene taking place, and Krystal sighed deeply. "Drama, act two, scene one..."

Sarah glanced up at the doorway of the dining hall through which both girls disappeared, praying everything would go well.

* * *

"Rachel, wait!" Chasmira cried as her friend prepared to round the corner.

Rachel froze, fists yet clenched, and turned, face fuming at Chasmira.

"I'm not gonna sit there and watch you two all giggly and enjoying yourself while Nathan just sits there like a lump—It's not fair that you get Aaron, get to parade around with him, then you exploit Eric in front of me, for the whole school to see, while Nathan just sits there and—"

"And how is Nathan being a timid boyfriend my fault?" she hissed, the hot tears streaming down her face. "He's *your* boyfriend."

Rachel opened her mouth then closed it, momentarily defeated. She shook, all the angrier for it, until Chasmira added, "Besides, you should be grateful you even have him. *I* don't have *any*one—"

"Oh, *come on*, you have Eric—"

"Is Eric Aaron? Could he ever be? Could he replace your Nathan? Or, by the sounds of things, maybe you don't even *care* about Nathan—"

"That's not fair—"

"Yeah? Well, neither was anything you just said to me. Maybe you should stop and think for a change. Maybe it's *you* who suck at being a friend..."

She whirled and stormed off, leaving Rachel standing hurt, angry, annoyed, about to fly up to her dorm room and kick a few, good holes in the walls, when Sarah's voice cut the air icily. "Uh-uh, sister. Don't you go *anywhere*."

Rachel turned, glaring. "I'm not in the mood for your self-righteous crud right now—"

"Which might be why you need it," Sarah snapped. "I saw pretty much all of what went on. What the heck *was* all that?"

"We were just having a disagreement—"

"Yelling and hissing like two alley cats, and, above all things, about *Eric Lindauer?* That hardly seems fitting, considering you have a boyfriend of your own, Rachel..."

"I...I, umm..." She looked away, frustratingly defeated once more.

"Look, I *know* what your problem is." Sarah grabbed Rachel by the arm, forcing the fuming red-head to look her in the eye. "But you should be grateful to still have Nathan at all, even if he *is* a dunderhead. Chasmira has *no* one. She has us, yes. But, well, you know what I mean. How would you feel if Nathan up and croaked and you found some other friend in whom you found solace and comfort, and suddenly, one of your other friends, presumably one of your best, began acting like a jerk because of something like childish jealousy? Because we all know that's what this is about, and I can assure you that Chasmira does *not* like Eric that way, and if she did, you have a man of your own, and so that's none of your business."

Rachel broke away from those accusing eyes. She took in a deep breath, trying to calm her own nerves. She had no right to get upset, not when she knew Sarah spoke the truth, not when she knew how much she hurt Chasmira who'd already been hurt nearly to the point of breaking, who didn't need any more hurt in her life to possibly shatter her heart altogether. She didn't need that at all. And yet, that's all she gave her in the past few days.

Taking in another deep breath, she looked up at Sarah sheepishly. "You're right. This has all been...stupid. And selfish of me. I need to apologize to Cassy and...I need to be there for her."

"She needs us *all* right now, Rachel," Sarah assured her. "Not just Eric, though she may be using him to fill a different kind of emotional gap right now. Remember that Aaron was her best *guy* friend before he was her boyfriend. She'll be missing that. But she still needs her girl friends. So go get her, Rachel."

Sarah grinned, and Rachel returned the smile. "Thanks."

"No problem, my wise rantings are free for the taking any time," Sarah assured as Rachel slipped from the hall.

CHAPTER 5

Rachel approached the garden, peering through the trees.

Chasmira lay on her back, staring with a vain hope in her eyes at the heavens, as though he might fall from the sky into her arms at any moment. A sharp pain stabbed at Rachel's heart. How could she have been so cruel to such a pitiful creature, and one she called her friend?

No room for guilt now, though. She must focus on Chasmira.

As she walked into the clearing, Chasmira looked over, surprise flashing in her eyes, and she sat up. "Hey, Rachel."

"Hey." She plopped down beside Chasmira whose eyes flashed painfully patient upon her own. Sighing, she looked down at the ground. "Look, Cassy. I know I've been a crummy friend these past few days. I need to apologize, and I need you to know it's not your fault, you don't deserve that with everything you're going through. I was just jealous...I used to have a thing for Eric, you know, and now he's paying you all that attention...I don't really still like him that way, I just wish Nathan, you know, would be at least a little bit like...Anyways, all this is no excuse for the way I've acted, and I'm really sorry. Forgiven?"

She looked up hopefully, and Chasmira smiled as best she could. "Forgiven."

Then she sighed and drew her gaze, as if magnetically, towards the white tombstone, the moon blossoms spilling all about it like a protective wreath. The tears leaped into her eyes, yet it seemed as if the grave held some gloomy enchantment over her mind. As if, because it was the last shred of him she possessed, she could do nothing but stare.

"Cassy...you wanna talk?"

"I'm just...confused," she breathed as the tears slipped quietly, gently down her cheeks.

Silence ensued. Rachel waited for her to continue.

"Rachel, Aaron was my first love, and yet, I believe, my only love. I've never cared about anyone so much or in that way, and I don't think I ever shall," Chasmira cried and laid her head on Rachel's shoulder. "I just miss him so much...I feel like a part of my own heart, my own soul, is missing, that part

80

which made me live, *want* to live...like only the part that can just survive remains."

Rachel gently stroked her hair. "Aaron was your first love, but perhaps he was not your true love, the one Amiel meant for you. I believe you'll love again, in time.

"I should have thought of this all sooner. I...I was just being selfish, and I'm sorry. If Eric loves you, you deserve another chance after all you've been through. And I should be grateful I still have Nathan."

"Nathan *can* be a dope," Chasmira sympathized, smiling feebly.

Rachel rolled her eyes. "Amen to that."

"But I think he'll come around, in time. I mean, you can't blame him for being so focused on his career, even if it *does* involve sitting around messing with computer games all day. And you can't really blame him either if the reason for his blundering is his infatuation with you."

"I guess." Rachel exhaled deeply, a playful twinkle entering her eyes. "You know, we could always have Sarah talk to him."

Chasmira laughed. "He'd *have* to take you on a proper date then, wouldn't he?"

Rachel smirked wryly, "Yes, by fear of death if he didn't, both by Sarah and me."

CHAPTER 6

Sarah entered the dorm room, plopping down her mound of books on the desk.

"Where's Chasmira?"

Rachel shrugged. "On a date or somethin' with Eric, I think."

"*What?*" hissed Sarah, eyes flashing.

"I apologized then told her to go for it."

"You did *what?*"

Rachel gazed at her confusedly. "Isn't this what you wanted? I apologized, Chasmira doesn't have to feel bad about pursuing him—"

"I said she shouldn't be afraid to be his friend, I said nothing *whatsoever*—"

"Oh, *come on.*" Krystal flounced from the bathroom, curls bouncing in an overly cutsie and thus overly annoying way in Sarah's mind. "It's all across the school how much he's head over heels for her. Don't you think it's a good thing for her, take her mind off of Aaron?"

"You really think she needs that right now? She's still sleeping with Aaron's paper clips under her pillow, crying herself to sleep each night. Need I go on?"

Rachel frowned. "No, that's exactly the point. Having Eric should be good for her—"

"He might be if she was ready! Don't you *get* it? If Nathan died, Rachel, or if Josh died, Krystal, or if Sam—"

"We're not dating," sang Hailey in an overly innocent yet threatening voice.

"Whatever. My point is, would you want someone shoving off some other guy on you? No, you wouldn't be ready..."

"But Chasmira's so...tender-hearted," Krystal decided. "She's falling apart. I think she needs someone there for her—"

Sarah threw her hands in the air. "Since when did that stop being *our* job?"

"Not *that* way, you *know* what we *mean*." Krystal sat on the edge of the bed in a perfect model stance which made Sarah more than want to spray her with something that would drown her curls and destroy her makeup. "Besides, Eric's a nicer guy than Aaron ever was."

"That's true," Rachel concurred.

"He *does* seem to be less of a dunderhead," Hailey added.

"Not to Chasmira," Sarah said seriously. "And, dare I say this aloud, not to *me* either. Maybe he thinks he's helping her as much as you all seem to think, but is he really?"

Rachel replied with a cool gaze. "We'll just have to wait and see, I guess."

Sarah narrowed her eyes, preparing to accept her challenge, when footsteps thudded down the hall, and with them, gasps for air and broken sobs. Sarah rushed to the door, poking her head out. As the noise receded, she drew back inside, hissing, "Well, way things are looking so far, I'm winning," before slipping out the door.

She rushed down the hallway and around the corner, but already Chasmira was out of sight, her pitiful sobs out of range. She must've kicked into high flying gear. Sarah leaped up also, soaring down the hallways—

"Umph!"

Rounding a corner, she crashed hard into something, bouncing back, skidding across the floor.

Standing, she glared as Eric stood to his feet.

"Sorry, Sarah." He brushed off his black suit coat. "Have you seen Chasmira?"

"Yeah, I saw her a few seconds ago," Sarah replied coldly.

"Did you see where she went?"

"She flew around the corner, crying her eyes out."

"What?" Concern illuminated his bright, blue eyes. "She said she was only going to the bathroom...I don't know what went wrong, we were just enjoying a nice dinner, talking..."

"What happened right before she went off to 'use the bathroom?'"

"We were talking casually about school, nothing serious. I offered her some green beans and she accepted, but a few moments after that, she sort of looked sick, ran off saying she had to use the bathroom, that she'd be right back..."

"You stupe!" Sarah snapped. "Green is Aaron's favorite color! Why would you offer her green beans?"

"I...I didn't know..." He stood looking very shameful for his stupidity, though he could not have known. "I didn't mean to cause so much trouble—"

"Yeah, but you sure seem to by your very presence," Sarah seethed.

Eric's eyes grew defensively cold. "Do you have a problem with my seeing Chasmira?"

"It depends upon how you are 'seeing her.' And we both know you pursue her as more than a friend, a shoulder to cry on in her time of need. That's just your way of getting to her."

"You make it sound like I'm using her." Anger tinged his voice, though he struggled to hold back any signs of this.

"Maybe you are and you just don't realize it."

"Chasmira *likes* spending time with me—"

"Oh, yes, and her crying outbreak was a clear sign of that—"

"An accident on my part, and one that won't happen again!"

"But how many others? How many 'accidents' do you think she can really take?"

"I can help her through it! She *needs* someone right now, *I* can be that person, *I* can help things seem less confused, let her know *I'm* here, that *I* love her —"

"Chasmira is still grieving, she can still barely drag herself from bed each morning because she's so distraught about losing Aaron. And you really think it's good, healthy, less confusing for her if you just butt in and try to take his place in her heart? You think you *can* take his place?"

Eric's face quickly flushed a violent red. The vein in his forehead pulsed, and he drew his lips very taut, forcing himself to take a deep breath. "If I can make it just a little bit easier for her to draw herself from bed, then, yes, I think it's worth it."

"And what happens when she realizes she's been dragging herself from bed for a big, fat nothing? When reality strikes and she realizes you were just a crutch, and as soon as that crutch is slipped from under her, what then? You think she won't fall even harder? You think someone will be able to catch her?"

"I won't *be* just a crutch," he seethed, his mask of patience quickly unraveling. "I *love* Chasmira."

"Then let her heal, give her time, and then, if she's ready, she'll know—"

"I can help her heal! What about that can't you understand?"

Sarah stared unblinking for some moments. She saw him flinch uncomfortably, but she took pity by breaking the silence. "I think it's *you* who doesn't understand. I think it's *you* who will understand too late. *I* know Chasmira. *You* don't. I don't think you're good for her—"

"I know her too. And I think I am."

"You would presume to know her better than her best friend since fifth grade knows her? Better than someone who can read her thoughts before she speaks them? But I won't stand in your way. And I won't stand in hers. If this is what you both think you need, want, whatever, I can't stop you. But don't say I didn't warn you."

Her eyes flashed coolly yet powerfully, triumphantly. He returned the gaze and said lowly, "There will be no need of such a reminder. I love Chasmira. I will prove it to her. I will prove it to her so clearly that she cannot help but love me in the end."

He whirled with a final glare, slipping around the corner and out of sight.

Sarah took in a deep breath. This was no time to allow herself to fume. Chasmira was what mattered right now, not her own self.

CHAPTER 7

Sarah entered the dorm room to find Chasmira sitting on the bed, legs scrunched close against her, head buried in her arms as she sobbed softly. Hailey was there too, only she seemed oblivious to the scene as she rummaged through her closet. *The others must've deserted*, Sarah thought, *when Chasmira stormed in all weepy-like. Or perhaps she requested their absence.* Either way, Hailey remained, as ever, absorbed in her own affairs.

"Thought I'd find you here when you weren't in the garden." Sarah sat on the bed beside her best friend, placing an arm around her.

"Sarah, I'm tired of crying, tired of being sad, tired of my heart being torn in two." Chasmira flopped down on her back.

Laying down next to her, Sarah asked gently, "Chasmira, this may seem like a very...blunt question, but...do you love Eric?"

"Has anyone seen my white sock?" chimed Hailey. "It's stretchy and goes up to my ankle."

"I don't know," Chasmira said softly. "That is, I *do* care about him, and I know he loves me, but...Sarah, I'm afraid..."

"Afraid?"

Hailey popped her head out of the closet, announcing to no one in particular she feared never finding her sock.

"Yes," Chasmira continued. "For a while, I was afraid to let go of Aaron, but now...now I'm mostly afraid to open up my heart to Eric. What if I fall in love with him and he leaves me too? Or what if, in loving Eric, I forget Aaron and what we shared?"

Chasmira looked up at Sarah with desperately longing eyes. "I so want to care about Eric as he does me, it's just that I'm afraid."

"I found it!" Hailey shouted.

"Shut up!" Sarah snapped before reaching into her pocket, pulling out her copy of the White Scrolls. Flipping to a marked passage, she handed it to Chasmira who read, "There is no fear in love; but perfect love casteth out fear: because fear hath torment. He that feareth is not made perfect in love."

86

Chasmira glanced up at Sarah who took her hand. "Perfect love casteth out fear; you cannot be afraid to love. Fear is not the issue. Have you prayed about this? Do you believe Amiel is leading you in this direction?"

In the background, Hailey mumbled something about the sock having a hole in it and smelling like rotten spinach.

"Yes," said Chasmira, quietly but firmly. "I've been praying."

"Then trust Amiel, and do not be afraid. Amiel is love, let Him cast out your fears. You cannot dwell on fear and forget to live."

"Thanks."

"Yeah, thanks for all your help in finding my sock," Hailey muttered sarcastically, holding up the smelly thing, totally unaware of the important conversation that just took place.

"*Would you stop griping?*" Sarah snarled. Hailey only stared at her, appalled at her rudeness, before leaving to take her poor sock down to the laundry room.

Sarah rolled her eyes, yet as soon as Hailey shut the door behind her, she turned to Chasmira, eyes glinting seriously. "One more thing, though. While fear shouldn't be an issue, well, there's just that. Are you sure this is the direction the Lord is leading you? I mean, I'm just not sure, though I know I'm not you..."

"Sarah, I know you're concerned, but this is what I want. I want someone. I can't have Aaron. It's that simple."

"Is it?"

Chasmira looked away from her powerfully skeptical glare.

"Chasmira, I've known you for a long time. And I know people. You know how I talk about my 'sixth sense' all the time. Well, it's true. I have a way of feeling people out. I'm not saying anything bad about him, I'm just saying...I don't know if he's your type."

"But maybe he is," she returned stubbornly. "And maybe by not giving him a chance I'd be missing out...or maybe I'm just confused...everyone thinks I should give him a chance, but now you say it might not be a good idea...but if I never do, then I'll never know, will I...?"

Sarah sighed. "I think you should try to ignore those other people and listen to what Amiel tells you in your heart. Shoot, ignore me even. This is *your choice* —I won't stand in your way. You wanna date Eric, go right ahead. I could be wrong about him anyways."

She shrugged and turned away, though Chasmira caught the yet skeptical glint in her eye. Sarah seldom thought herself wrong about this sort of thing, and she seldom was. And if Chasmira planned on listening to any outside advice, should she not listen to that of the best friend who never steered her wrong before?

Still, despite the doubt hammering dully inside her mind—a doubt she excused as nothing more than her inner fears at everything, both pain and the chance for a new love being so fresh, so frightful—she determined in her mind there could be no harm in trying. She would try to love Eric just as much as he loved her, and, Amiel-willing, succeed.

CHAPTER 8

The months passed, and Chasmira grew slowly yet steadily closer to Eric, came to rely upon him, trust him, feel secure in him, even to love him. They became known as the most beautiful couple on campus, destined for greatness, beloved even by Rachel who tried to remain calm long enough in Nathan's presence one evening so that he was finally able to speak to her without sounding like a bumbling buffoon, asking her out on a proper date.

Christmas dawned, and they all gathered in the girls' dorm, hauling their presents for each other along with them. Christmas was the one time the ban on traveling to the opposite sex's dorms was truly and officially lifted.

After ripping into several gifts, paper, ribbons and glow-in-the-dark bows, courtesy of Josh White, lay strewn on the ground. Even Nate and Lucy joined the gathering, nuzzling each other in a corner Hailey refused to look at, as though the affection radiating from the spot might curse her with blindness if she stole even a glance.

Sarah handed a smallish box to Chasmira.

"Before you open my gift, I should warn you. I started making it several months ago and...if it upsets you, I apologize, and you don't have to keep it..."

Chasmira had already removed the wrapping paper.

She smirked. "Wow, another box."

"And not just any other box, but a genuine shoe box," added Josh.

Chasmira opened the box and pulled out a crocheted scarf. It was sage green.

"I know you said you weren't wearing green anymore because of you-know-who...his favorite color," Sarah began awkwardly, studying her guiltily.

But Chasmira smiled, though a bit sadly. "It's beautiful. Besides, sage green is one of my favorite colors, and—" She glanced shyly at Eric but quickly turned away as she felt herself blush. "—green is also one of Eric's favorite colors, along with silver, so I'm wearing it again."

Rachel sat in bewildered silence that such a shade of green called "sage" existed. How did she never read about this? She would have to stop slacking on her trips to the library...

Sarah looked relieved then beamed.

"Silver? Oh, then my other gift is perfect."

Her other gift was a pair of silver, heart earrings. Chasmira heartily thanked her as Eric helped her don them.

Several more gifts were exchanged, including a bottle of perfume from Josh to Krystal. She rushed continuously to the bathroom, expecting her skin to turn green or fall off any second, though Josh continually reassured her the perfume was not jinxed.

Nathan gave Rachel a book on unicorns, and she would've hugged him but thought better of his poor nerves.

Sam, meanwhile, handed a box of tacks to Hailey.

"What?" She glared defensively as everyone stared at them confusedly. "Everyone collects something, don't they?"

Finally, one gift remained, hidden within a red, sparkling gift bag.

"Who...?" began Nathan, but then Eric picked it up, presenting it to Chasmira who received it with a quick intake of breath. As she realized she must be staring at him like he possessed ten heads, she recovered, managing, "Thank you."

Eric smiled. Must he smile so much? It made her blush terribly, suddenly at a loss for words.

"Aren't you going to open it?" he mused.

"Oh! Yes..."

Reaching inside the tissue paper, she pulled out a beautiful snow globe, causing everyone, even the guys, to stare and gasp in awe.

Inside stood three pine trees, stars floating about them, silver stars magically suspended in the air. The most captivating feature was the intense realness of the landscape. The base of the snow globe glowed green and silver, elegantly carved, and on top perched a jolly snowman.

Turning it over, Chasmira espied a silver knob.

No sooner did her fingers brush the knob than Eric cried, "No! Wait!"

She jumped, drawing her hand back sharply, staring at him.

He blushed this time. "I'm sorry. I should have told you. It's an antique. I meant to get it repaired but ran out of time, so the song doesn't play quite yet, but it will, soon as I can take it in to be fixed. So please, 'til then, it's best if you don't try to play it or shake it."

"It's okay. It's still beautiful."

"Indeed." His eyes glittered deeply into hers. Unease caused her hands to shake, so she quickly set the snow globe in her lap, saying quietly, "Thank you."

"You're very welcome."

"I'm sorry...I didn't think to get you anything."

"You don't need to—seeing your eyes come to life was enough of a gift."

She smiled again while Sarah elbowed Rachel who sighed dreamily. Hailey made a barfing motion at Sam who stifled a laugh.

"Well, enough of this gushy stuff," Josh sniffed. "Let's go down to the hall for some of that unlimited hot chocolate."

"Okay." Krystal eyed him warningly. "But nothing unlimited for you or you'll be trying to drag me into the men's bathroom with you every ten seconds having to pee like you did the other day."

"Oh, heh, heh, that was just a crummy plan to get you to make out with me someplace we haven't yet. I don't really have such an unmanageable bladder."

"*Okay*," said Rachel loudly, standing. "Let's go before the conversation grows any more inappropriate."

Chasmira smiled shyly as Eric offered his hand. She hesitated then took it. It closed firmly around her own as he led her alongside the others towards the promise of hot chocolate.

* * *

As the day came to an end, everyone retired to their dorm rooms.

"Chasmira, can I talk to you for a sec?" Eric asked as everyone else filed their separate ways.

"Certainly."

He drew her into a quiet hallway before facing her and whispering, "Chasmira, I must tell you something about that snow globe I gave you today."

Chasmira gazed into his eyes, waiting curiously for him to reveal the deep mystery their blue depths concealed. A hint of unrest flowed beneath their sparkle.

"I told you not to shake it or play the song because it's such an old antique," he continued in a hushed voice. "Well, that's not true, I mean, it *is* very old, but..."

He glanced up at the ceiling as if searching for an escape.

"Dang, how do I say this?" His eyes pleaded her for relief.

"Chasmira, I have to go away again for a while."

Hurt flashed across her face.

"Cassy, please, I know you don't understand right now, but someday you will. I need you to trust me."

"I do..." she promised quietly.

"Now listen carefully. Where I am going, it is very dangerous. The snow globe is a portal to where I'm going. If you turn the knob all the way and turn it over seven times, you'll be transported to me. However, no matter how much you may miss me, you must promise not to use the snow globe unless you are in trouble. But if danger should come to you, use it at once, for although it is treacherous where I am going, you would be in more danger if you remained here, should that danger ever follow you."

She frowned, searching his troubled eyes, breathing, "What danger? What are you talking about?"

He sighed, forcing a feeble smile as he caressed her face. "Nothing for you to ever worry about, Amiel willing. Just trust me and know that I will keep you safe whether we are together or apart."

"I trust you," she confirmed again.

"And I love you, with all my heart."

She took in a sharp breath, gazing up at him guiltily, trying to force the words which stubbornly refused to surface, to feel quite right as her mind echoed them.

"It's okay." He kissed her forehead. "I know this is all new to you, like starting over. You don't have to be ready."

Smiling reassuringly, he took her hand. "I must go."

She nodded as a tear slipped down her cheek. He brushed it gently aside then lifted her hand to his lips, kissing it softly. "'Til we meet again, my princess."

Then he turned and slipped around the corner. She hesitated a moment before rushing after him. But upon rounding the corner, he had vanished from sight.

CHAPTER 9

It was another, normal, Friday evening. Chasmira, Rachel, Josh, Krystal, Nathan, Sam, Hailey, and Sarah all gathered in one of the libraries. All the girls were reading, except Hailey who sat on the window seat, gazing at the stars, while Chasmira engrossed herself in Nathan's and Josh's chess game. Josh was losing badly, continuously shouting things like, "Aww, man!", "No, not my other knight!", and, "Nathan, I think you're cheating. Are you sure that's even legal?" The librarian swept by several times, hissing warnings at Josh and threatening to kick him out.

Nathan snatched Josh's bishop, leaving Josh with only his king and two pawns. Nathan still owned all his pieces save a few pawns, a bishop, and a knight. He allowed Josh to take his knight just to be nice, and Josh celebrated in a victory dance that won him another nasty glare from the librarian.

Josh was just complaining about being knocked down to one pawn when all the lights went out. They all jumped in surprise, and Krystal screamed. Josh hissed, "Man, Nathan, that's a little extreme, don't you think? I mean, you're already winning, no need to cheat further, rub it in...dirty, cheaty, cheat-face..."

Suddenly, Pastyre Saltzgiver's voice sounded over the speakers, "No one panic. I'm sure it's just a brief power outage."

"Why...?" muttered Rachel. "In a magic school, *why* electricity...?"

Everyone was silent until Hailey mused, "That's odd. The stars seem to be going out too."

Gazing out the window, they saw the stars indeed fading. The sky inked pitch black until they could see nothing. Never had they known such darkness, and uncontrollable chills rippled up their spines.

"Does anyone have a light pebble?" someone asked.

Almost everyone wore one around their neck or had one shoved in their pockets, they were each supposed to have one with them at all times in case of emergency, and pulled them out, activating them by tapping three times. The pebbles glistened and illuminated the room a bit. However, it was still very dark, shadowy, and creepily ominous.

A long, uneasy silence ensued, until Pastyre Saltzgiver's voice boomed again over the speakers, this time very urgently, "Everyone arm yourselves and head immediately to the dining hall! The school is under attack! I repeat, arm yourselves and make for the dining hall!"

Everyone sprang up and rushed from the library.

"Everyone keep together now and keep calm," ordered the librarian.

They made their way carefully in the near total darkness. Everyone was prepared to shoot fire, ice, lightning, or whatever was necessary in order to defend themselves against the unknown foe. Sam summoned his, Josh's, and Nathan's old swords to them, and they led the way beside the librarian, while the others held up the pebbles which seemed to offer little light or hope in that incredible darkness.

The librarian held up a hand, and everyone stopped abruptly before the fork in the hallway.

"Did you hear that?" she breathed.

"Hear what?" Josh whispered.

"I heard *some*thing," Nathan said.

"Shh, there it is again," Sam silenced them.

Everyone froze. A chilling chorus of continual hisses rose and fell, rose and fell, flesh sliding across flesh, clicking softly, softly, yet eerily, an unknown, fearful sound. The chorus continued its terrible song, culminating in volume, intensity, 'til finally the librarian dared to unsheathe her pebble and hold it up in cupped hands.

"Oh my," she breathed.

Chasmira clutched Rachel's hand.

On the wall before them hung the huge painting of the lion and the lamb, or what once was that picture. Within the frame teemed hundreds of immense, slithering, hissing serpents, red, wild eyes alight with a mad fury.

"Run and arm yourselves!" the librarian shrieked. The next moment, the serpents lunged. The air rained with the slithery enemies as they emerged from the painting. Lightning sparks and jets of flame rebounded off walls, ceiling, and floor as several people tried to shield everyone as they raced past the painting, stumbling over each other and over the serpents themselves. Screams and vengeful hisses swirled in the air, darkness blinded, adding to the confusion. Several held out their pebbles but others did not want to see. Yet soon all could not help but see as hundreds of red eyes loomed at them from the blackness, surrounding them, ghost-like as the invisible bodies reached for their ankles, invisible fangs lurching for their flesh.

Some flew, some ran as quickly as they could from that hallway, the serpents all the while pursuing. As they passed the other paintings on the walls, they could see by the brief illumination of the librarian's and others' pebbles, countless serpents pouring from them as well. Cataclysmic madness encompassed as serpents soared through the air, exploding as lightning, fire, and other magic attacks struck them. The snakes coiled around the feet of the flightless like a tangled web. The fairies were forced to lift the elves into the air and carry them to keep them from being drowned in the horrible mass of scales, skin, and venomous fangs.

Suddenly, Mr. Root shot around the corner, shouted some loud, undecipherable words, and instantly, the serpents froze, paralyzed, and fell limp at their feet.

"Hurry to the dining hall!"

They all rushed down the next hallway and down another flight of stairs. At the bottom, another, huge serpent leered up at them, but Mr. Root quickly dispatched of it with a zap of lightning. He kept his hand hovered over the snake, streaks of electric white emanating from his fingertips and causing the snake to writhe and twist in pain.

"Tell me, beast," hissed Mr. Root, "where do you come from? Whom do you serve, and whom do you seek?"

The serpent hissed a final, inaudible word, glaring with a last, defiant glint before he fell lifeless before them. Mr. Root growled in frustration.

Then, they espied more pairs of eager eyes, gleaming with a vengeance, rounding the corner and surging straight towards them.

"Everyone to the dining hall!" Mr. Root shouted, sending several volleys into the midst of the serpents.

"Where's Chasmira?" Rachel shrieked.

Chasmira alone understood the serpent's dying word—Eriz. Her own name. They were seeking her. Eric's words flooded back to her. They were all in danger, and now she knew the danger loomed near because of her own self. She must get to him, seek his aid.

As she rushed back up the stairs, she could feel the serpents pursuing her, could almost hear the angry rhythms of their hearts, though she dare not glance back into those hungry eyes. More rushed from the hallway as she breached the top of the steps. Those Mr. Root had paralyzed now awakened. More than a hundred serpents trailed her heels, yet she had no time to fight back nor strength enough to defy them all. She flew faster than ever before to her dorm room and slammed the door shut behind her. Reaching for the glittering snow globe, frantically turning the knob all the way, the gentle music began to play. She turned the snow globe over once—

Something banged violently against the door, and she jumped, staring in horror, frozen.

A second turn, three, four, five, six—

The door crashed down and the serpents flooded in, eyes blazing, hisses echoing vehemently in a terrible, deafening chorus. One of them whipped its tail around, knocking the snow globe from her trembling fingers. Another wrapped itself tightly around her body and began to squeeze, hard. As her breath escaped her, she began to grow unconscious. But, no, she must get the snow globe. Levitating a nearby lamp with the last ounce of her conscious, she conked the serpent hard over the head. Stunned, it released its grasp on her. She dropped to the ground, safe for a half second as all the serpents encircled her, rearing back their heads to strike. She dove for the snow globe, snatched it up, and turned it over a seventh time—

CHAPTER 10

Immediately, she felt her body being jerked in all directions, and she wondered if she had failed and the serpents now tore her apart as the unusual though painless feeling gripped her. But then the pull stopped, and while darkness still surrounded her, it was a peaceful, still darkness. Tiny diamonds—stars —glittered as far as she could see. Gradually, she became aware of cool air filling her lungs, the cold, hard surface beneath her body. Sitting up at last, she took in her breath.

A little, wooded clearing encompassed her, snow glittering upon the encircling pine trees. Standing, she walked over to one of the trees, running her fingers over the trunk whose bark was not a rough brown but a smooth silver. She smiled, eyes glittering in wonder.

For some time, she stood drinking in a beauty of the still, serene wood. But as a light snow began to fall, she shivered, realizing the stark coldness and vainly hugging herself in hopes of finding warmth, wishing for Sarah's sage green scarf.

Glancing about, she wondered what to do. It was useless to just stand here, and yet, where should she go? Where *could* she go? She did not even hold the faintest clue of where she was. She prayed Amiel might show her the way and especially that He would protect those she left behind, desiring none to get hurt, especially on her own account.

The silence, which at first covered her like a soothing blanket, now began to stifle her with uneasiness, a fearsome aloneness. The unease gripped her even more as the quiet was broken by a branch snapping. She jumped up in an attempt to fly from the clearing, but she only crashed hard to the ground. Scrambling up, she leapt into the air with the same results. Panic gripped her heart. Why couldn't she fly? An ominous knowing overcame as she attempted to shoot ice at a nearby tree. Nothing happened, save the mocking howl of the wind echoing through the trees, which seemed themselves no longer inviting but a like a cage entrapping her...

As a shadow slipped by in the trees, she froze, waiting for whatever was about to strike, heart sickened as it knew waiting was all she possessed in her power to do—

From the shadows of the trees leapt three creatures screeching hideously. Giant lizards, standing as tall as men, poised, erect on hind legs ready to spring at any moment, muscular as giants she read of but never dared hope to encounter. Crimson and ebony armor glinted upon their black-scaled bodies, black swords and shields glittered darkly in the light of the stars and moon. The light reflected too upon the snow, which now seemed dim and tainted.

"Surrender the crown," one of the beasts hissed, cruel claws clenching the hilt of his cold, curved blade.

"I don't know what you're talking about," she cried desperately, beyond hope of sounding brave as she glanced helplessly into each of their cruelly gleaming eyes. "I *have* no crown—you have the wrong person!"

"Are you not the Princess of Destiny Future?" another hissed lowly, ominously, as though knowing she already knew the answer.

"Y-yes, I am," she breathed.

Her heart fell into a bottomless pit as the lizard smirked, nodding his head while never allowing his eyes to stray from her. Then, as the three surged towards her, she stood trembling, praying. What else could she do? Fear froze her feet to the icy ground, and she possessed no other means of defending herself.

The lizards were mere inches from her side when something streaked past with lightning-swiftness in a silver blur, knocking all three of the lizard warriors in the head in turn, and yet so quickly it seemed to happen all at once. The silver thing then zoomed back into the trees from which it flew. Looking down, she saw the three lizards lying fallen, clustered around her feet. She did not know whether they were dead or merely stunned. She knew only a sudden weariness as she sank to her knees, sobbing with relief, releasing the overwhelming fear welling inside her.

A hand touched her shoulder, and she gasped. Dare she glance up to see who owned that hand? Even if the person just saved her life, that person may still be a foe. But then a gentle voice said, "They're dead now. They will bring you no more harm."

She gasped again, stood, turned, then stared upon him in wonder, wonder that he stood before her at all, then wonder at how magnificently he stood before her, clad in white blouse, silver tunic, darker silver pants, and shining black boots studded with onyx stones. In one hand, he clutched the silver boomerang which slew the lizards, and the silver hilt of a sword glimmered in a sheath hung about his waist.

When she found herself able to breathe, her momentary awe at his kingly appearance passing, reality drowned her once more, and she threw her arms around him, crying all over again. His strong arms closed tenderly about her, one hand curving securely about her waist, the other reaching up to stroke her hair ever so comfortingly. They stood this way until she again caught her breath and released the much-needed tears, until his touch calmed her trembling heart. Then, as they faced each other, his hands clasping the small of her back, he lifted one hand to brush a tear from her cheek, asking gently yet seriously, "Are you alright? Besides being frightened, of course."

"Yes," she answered, quietly but firmly.

"When did you get here?"

"Only a few minutes ago. Eric, the school, it's under siege—"

"I know. I've already sent others to help them destroy the serpents. They'll be okay."

Chasmira stared. "How did you know—?"

"Not now." Eric glanced about cautiously. "And not here. I've a camp a few miles from here. We'll rest there tonight, and, in the morning, I'll explain everything."

As he took her hand, he led her out of the clearing, into the depths of the woods, which once again shone peacefully. All fear dissolved as his presence touched the wood. Gazing up at him admiringly, she asked, "Can you at least tell me how it is you were able to find me so quickly?"

"As soon as I heard the school was under siege, I rushed to the clearing as fast as I could. I knew you'd arrive there soon, or I hoped. I'm sorry I didn't get there sooner myself, in fact."

"I'm just glad you came when you did. It was hard for me to leave the others in danger, but I knew the serpents were looking for me, so I thought it might be safer for the others if I left, like you said."

"Yes, they should be taken care of by now, and if the serpents know you are no longer at the school, no more should be dispatched there.

"Here we are..."

As they entered another, small clearing, Chasmira gasped. In one tree perched a beautiful barn owl, and beneath the tree stood the most elegant, wondrous creature she ever beheld. It was a horse with a pure, white, glistening coat and mane. Its eyes and hooves shimmered silver.

"Eric, is that—is that really a zilchus?"

"Yes." He smiled at her enthusiasm. "Silverswift, a descendant of Flashling herself."

Chasmira noted a shield resting against one of the trees. It too shone silver, bearing the Lozolian coat of arms—a golden sword within a golden cross. But were they really still in Loz? It certainly wasn't winter at the school. Perhaps they were further south, close to the Icean Mountains. Yet, as she yawned, she realized how sleepy she was, deciding not to worry about feeding her curiosity 'til morning, as Eric promised.

CHAPTER 11

"I hope you're still not afraid of heights." Eric smiled up at Chasmira as he stored the remainder of food into the packs carried by the zilchus. They had just shared a breakfast of eggs, bread, and fresh spring water. Eric declared they best be off. The day held many tasks to accomplish.

"I wasn't afraid until my flying powers disappeared."

He gazed confusedly at her for a moment, heart radiating with compassion as she glanced around the woods with a doubtful, frightened gleam yet reflected in her eyes. Then a sudden realization flashed upon his face as he exclaimed, "Oh! I forgot. You see, she has placed a spell on the land that robs everyone who sets foot here of their special powers. I meant to bring you a gem that counters the spell but completely forgot it in my haste. I apologize, but I promise to get you one as soon as we reach the palace."

"The palace?"

He felt gladdened as she cocked her head in that familiar, child-like, curious stance.

"And who is...*she?*"

"We should make haste, but I'll tell you along the way."

He helped Chasmira onto Silverswift's back and climbed on behind her, commanding the zilchus to head for the palace. The horse sprinted through the woods at an amazing speed. Everything whisked by in a smooth, silver-white blur. The next moment, they rose just as smoothly, gently, and yet more swiftly, high above the treetops, Eric declaring, "It's much safer to travel by air, for all of her spies and servants are on land."

"And will you tell me now who 'her' is?"

He laughed lightly. "Indeed." His eyes glinted with a grave glimmer. "She is the evil lady who has been attacking Loz with the great snakes, lizards, and other monsters she has under her command. Her name and origin are unknown, but she is called 'The Dark Lady' or 'Princess of the Night' by her followers."

"Loz? Are we really still in Loz?"

"Yes, see for yourself. We approach the Lozolian Palace even now."

THE SECRET SISTER AND THE SILVER KNIGHT

As they flew over a high hill, Chasmira took in a sharp breath. Before them stretched the Crystal Lake, and situated on an isle in its midst towered the grand Lozolian Palace, just as she read about in her history books.

Soaring over the outer wall, passing the courtyard's threshold, they landed next to the stables and dismounted. Eric began to lead Silverswift into one of the stables, while Chasmira asked excitedly, "But how can this be? I thought the palace was destroyed years ago."

Eric shook his head. "No. When Loz, being part of those islands once known as 'Zephyr's,' became a part of the United States, we gradually adopted their traditions, pledging loyalty to their leader. The U.S. government never forbid us from keeping our own leader, only we had no need of a queen or king—'til now. Part of the historical Loz was preserved, your snow globe being one of the portals here. You see, there was a prophecy that when evil rose up in Loz once more, after the Second Age of the Dragon passed, the Princess of Destiny must take her place as the final queen of Loz and lead her people to peace once more. Come, let me show you something."

Taking her hand, he led her through a side door inside the palace. They passed no one save a few guards who nodded respectfully at their passing. A quiet serenity hung about the place, along with a silent waiting.

As they came to two golden doors ornately carved with the Lozolian crest, the two guards standing on either side swung them slowly inward. Eric led her inside as she again stared speechless and wondering. From the tall, stain-glass windows to the elegant tapestries to the rich marble floors and pillars, it was the most magnificent room she ever laid eyes upon. But her attention quickly focused upon a golden throne set with a purple velvet cushion, perched proudly atop a dais at the far end of the room. Eric smiled as he beheld her wonderment, and then, his hand yet in hers, he led her towards it.

"The throne that stands before you has stood empty for hundreds of years. Yet it now belongs to you."

Chasmira stared up at him, shaking her head incredulously. "But why me?"

"You are the Princess of Destiny, yes?"

She could only ogle at him, and then at the throne, blinking as the impossible reality tried to dawn upon her but couldn't quite. She nearly forgot that title 'til today. This was all too great to be real.

"Let me show you something else," he continued, this time in a very low voice, "but you must promise to share the secret with no one."

"I promise," she breathed.

He led her to the throne which was all the more magnificent to behold up close, then led her around behind it. They faced its smooth, golden back as he leaned close and whispered, "Nepo, nepo, nepo. The Princess of Destiny is come."

It seemed that either the throne grew or the two of them shrunk, and the lines of a door carved in the gold back of the throne appeared before their eyes. As Eric clasped the golden handle, turning it and leading Chasmira within, she found herself wondering if the amazing string of surprises would ever end.

They traipsed down a long, winding staircase. The way was dark save for the steps themselves which glowed with a dim light. Finally, at the bottom rose a door bearing the emblem of the golden sword within the golden cross. Eric carefully stooped, slipping a golden key from his boot, and opened the door. They stepped inside a small, dark room. From the far end shone a white, bright light. Hovering before them was the most radiant crown. It was made of pure, golden roses woven together, some of them rose-gold, some yellow, some white, all emanating a heavenly, hopeful sparkle.

"This," Eric announced reverently, "is the most precious treasure Loz now holds and protects. It is this the Dark Lady seeks, for whoever wears this crown on her head shall be queen of Loz. That is why she sought you out at the school and why I've been traveling here, trying to keep her forces at bay and from breaking past our barriers into your world to attack. She wishes to destroy you, keep you from having any chance at the throne, and claim the crown for her own self."

"But why could I not wear the crown *now*, become queen? Would that not stop her?"

"No, for she would seek your life still, and what's more, according to the prophecy, one of the last made by Zephyr before she died, when the Princess of Destiny and the Princess of the Night both fight for the crown, one must die before the other can become queen. There is a magical, binding force on this crown that will allow neither of you to become queen until one or the other is utterly defeated."

Fear settled over her, extinguishing wonder and excitement as the gravity of the situation this beautifully glittering object hovering before her suddenly descended.

Eric squeezed her hand. "Trust me, it is *you* who shall be victorious, and I will be at your side every step of the way. *I promise*."

She turned to search his bright, blue eyes. Their sincerity was illuminated by the scintillating waves of the crown's glow, and she smiled, taking in a deep breath. He grinned in return. "Come. We have one other duty to fulfill."

He led her then to another door, and as they opened it, Chasmira peered inside to see a large, triangular table set up in the midst of a triangular stone room. Knights and dames clad similarly to Eric stood before their high-backed chairs, around the perimeter of the table.

"Good morning, Sir Lindauer," greeted one knight as Eric entered.

"You're late," teased another.

Eric smiled. "And for good reason." He turned to Chasmira who stood back timidly in the doorway. "Come. You have nothing to fear here."

As she took his outstretched hand, he led her to the two empty chairs on the far side of the table. She blushed as she passed each knight and dame who stared upon her in wonder before bowing their heads respectfully.

As Eric and Chasmira took their seats beside each other, the knights and dames following suit, the knight to Chasmira's left turned to her. "Long has your chair sat empty, my lady. We rejoice in this day that it is filled again."

Chasmira smiled, nodding her head humbly, still too over-awed to utter a word.

"I call this meeting of the Lozolian Knights to order," Eric declared. "Let us open with prayer."

After Eric thanked Amiel for this time to come together and meet once more, especially thanking Him for Chasmira's presence and safety, and after asking Amiel's blessing on their meeting as they planned for the war to come, he announced, "As you can all see, I have brought the Lady Chasmira, our destined queen, here to meet with us today. Let us first each introduce ourselves."

The knight on Chasmira's left rose and placed a hand firmly to his heart. "I am Sir David, my lady, and I offer you my service, in life or in death."

His eyes gazed deeply into hers, glinting sincerely.

Next to him arose Mariah, who spoke with a gentle voice, and next to her rose another knight, Steven. As each of them stood and pledged their service to Chasmira, she studied their beautiful blue blouses, their blue and silver tunics, the Lozolian coat of arms stitched nobly upon their breasts. She wondered why Eric's attire alone looked so different, stood out so. But most of all, she noticed in each of their eyes shone that same, sincere and hopeful light. Each of them touched their heart not merely as some light ritual but because their hearts truly belonged to her. They gave them freely.

Once all the knights and dames had introduced themselves and sat back down, David asked with a playful glimmer in his eye, "And aren't you going to introduce yourself, Sir Lindauer?"

Eric smiled at David, then at Chasmira as he stood, taking one of her slender hands in his own, clasping the other firmly over his heart. "Sir Lindauer, the Silver Knight and thus head of the Council of Lozolian Knights, and therefore, I, above all, do pledge my unyielding loyalty, promising ever to stand by your side."

Chasmira smiled shyly at him as David added, "The Silver Knight is a most honorable title, one he's borne well for three years now."

"Enough gloating on my behalf, David." Eric took his seat, exchanging a grin with David who nodded. "Let's get started, shall we?

"Mariah, our faithful spy in matters concerning the war, has told us that the Dark Lady has been gathering troops to herself, according to the conversation overheard by some of her servants. Of course, it would be most helpful to know where she and her headquarters are located, but...anyway, she has broken through the south portal into the college grounds, and, of course, we've sent reinforcements there to stop them. Any word there?"

"Yes, my lord, I received word only moments ago from Professor Root," announced a dame known as Lady Katrina. "The serpents have all been vanquished and no more continue to arrive, nor shall they. Apparently, the Dark Lady used her shape-shifting powers to transform all the paintings and other drawings into portals. Windows, if you will, into the school, and it was through them the serpents entered. Pastyre Saltzgiver, Professor Root, and others figured this out and have been able to successfully seal up all these portals so none may enter by them again."

Eric nodded. "Very good. Thank you, Lady Katrina. And, if you would, once the Council meeting is over, please assure them of Lady Chasmira's safety here."

"Yes, Sir Lindauer."

"Thank you. Now, has anyone heard from the Washandzees or Wookies?"

"The Washandzees are still on our side," answered David. "However, the Wookies are being stubborn and remain neutral—as ever."

"Hmm..." mused Steven. "Neutral? No one will be able to remain neutral once the war breaks out."

"Excuse me." Chasmira frowned, intrigued despite her shyness. "I don't mean to interrupt, but what exactly are we talking about?"

"Certainly, my lady, it is as important for you to know the plans of your own kingdom's defense as anyone," said David patiently. "The Dark Lady is planning a war against the Lozolian Palace in hopes to take the crown, that is, if she could find it. Of course, she does not have the key nor the magic words necessary to enter the crown's chamber. Still, her first step in reaching it is taking the palace for her own."

"We've been gathering troops to our side," Eric continued, "trying to get as many peoples of and surrounding Loz to follow us. We've gathered many allies, but so has she. However, we seem to be strongest in numbers, though we lack other important information such as where her headquarters are actually located."

"Are they invisible?" Chasmira suggested.

"Possibly. We have our best magical scouts surveying all of Loz right now, searching. We know it has to be here, right under our noses probably. We just have to find it."

No one spoke for a moment, only watching their leader, waiting for further instruction.

At last, he said, "Well, gentlemen, ladies, I believe it is important we all get a good night's rest, especially our princess here. Meeting dismissed."

Everyone rose, bidding Chasmira good-night as they filed out. Eric and Chasmira were last to leave as he announced he would lead her to the room long prepared for her, for when this day arrived.

Eric stopped her before a closed door. "Get a good night's rest. We'll leave early in the morning. There are some more things I'd like to show you."

Chasmira frowned. "In the morning? But tomorrow is Monday. Shouldn't we—?"

Eric placed a finger to her lips to interrupt her protest. "I know you don't like to miss school. However, all the school staff knows the importance of your destiny, as will your fellow students, in time. For all they know, I might be keeping you for weeks to explain things to you, so I'm sure they won't miss you if you're gone a few days."

Chasmira pondered. Normally, she would rant at the prospect of missing a single moment of class. But now things were so changed. Some time away from school, a new place, a different feel, it might all do her well. Even though she was, in a sense, closer to danger remaining here in the palace, the target of the Dark Lady's efforts, she somehow felt safer, more secure here with Eric, away from the constant reality of school life. Here was like a fairy tale, a dream, one she was not quite ready to wake up from, for she'd been weary and in need of such a peaceful sleep for a long time.

The matter decided, another thought slowly occurred to her, and she looked up at him curiously. "I suppose I wouldn't mind staying for a few days. But, tell me, how is it that *you* haven't fallen behind in your school work? You leave for weeks, months even, and yet you're right on track when you return."

"I usually take several weeks' worth of assignments with me, keep in touch with Mr. Root, send in assignments through magic as I complete them, and he helps me keep on task."

Chasmira smiled. "And Rachel says you're lazy."

He shrugged. "Used to be. Still am, in some ways. It's hard to be lazy though lately, with so much to do with the Council."

Silence fell for a few moments. He stepped closer until he towered right over her. Her breath quickened as he gazed deeply into her eyes, tenderly caressing the curls that framed her face. "Well, good night. I'll see you in the morning."

"Good night, Eric," she breathed.

She trembled as he kissed her forehead. He blushed as she smiled.

He turned, slipping down the hall, receding from view. Then she slipped into her room.

Again, she drew in her breath. The furniture was richly constructed of a gorgeous, light oak. Purple silks strung about the four posts of the canopy bed. The gauzy curtains themselves were a pale pink embroidered with sage, aqua, and purple butterflies. So he remembered her favorite colors, as well as the fact that she loved butterflies. A strange specialness fluttered in her stomach as she walked over to the wardrobe. Opening wide the doors, of which more butterflies made their painted home, she found the wardrobe full of beautiful gowns embroidered, studded with glitter and gems and laces—all reflections of her feminine, elegant side.

She selected a white night dress embroidered with tiny, white flowers and snuggled beneath the covers of the huge bed. How warm and soft, incredibly so.

THE SECRET SISTER AND THE SILVER KNIGHT

As she closed her eyes, breathing her prayers, she smiled contentedly, wondering what new discovery Eric held in store tomorrow.

CHAPTER 12

Chasmira could describe the breakfast shared the next morning with Eric and some of the other knights and dames of the council as both hearty and amusing. The food itself tasted scrumptious. A long table stretched, piled high with every breakfast food that could ever be conceived. However, Charlie, one of the knights who drug himself rather groggily in, complained the eggs could use some more pepper, and after finding the pepper shaker empty, muttered something in frustration and chucked it out the nearby window.

After this interesting little escapade, Eric led Chasmira down to the stables where Silverswift awaited them.

As they flew once more over the woods, Chasmira asked, "So, where are we going today?"

"I thought I would show you some of my favorite places here in Ancient Loz. Would you like that?"

"Yes, very much so. Where are we going first?"

"How would you like to see the garden once owned and kept by Amanda Danielle?"

"I'd love to! But...will anything be growing there in winter?"

"The garden is still protected with all sorts of magic, tended regularly by faithful fairies and elves. It is kept warm and the plants preserved magically all year round, many of which are used to make many of our medicines, foods, and other important items.

"Look. There's the garden now."

Chasmira espied the hedge wall running about the perimeter of the Garden of Endless Lights. The white watch tower jutted out from the corner where two of the walls met. Chasmira saw the outline of someone watching in the window, just as Aaron described it so seemingly long ago.

They flew up to the tower where a beautiful young Mira girl greeted them at the window with a curtsy.

"Good morning, Sir Lindauer." She beamed at them. "And to you, my lady."

"May we enter the garden?" Eric asked.

"Yes, go right ahead." Her eyes twinkled playfully. "The roses have just opened, you know. They're quite beautiful. I would be certain to visit that spot."

"Thank you, Kierra, daughter of Liv."

Eric led Silverswift over the wall into the garden.

"But I thought we had to enter by the tower," Chasmira said.

"By land, yes, but those whom the lady at the tower wills may enter from the sky. Though the inner garden where the Lights are kept is now protected by the invisible yet undeniable barrier of light and truth that does not allow those with evil and untrue hearts to enter."

Silverswift swooped downward at Eric's command, into a little clearing, and Eric helped Chasmira off the horse. She smiled as all about them bloomed beautiful roses of all colors and shades—in the lofty trees, in the full bushes, dew drops glittering delicately upon their every petal like tiny, pure diamonds. Never did so many roses gather in one place, never did so many roses ensnare the senses with their beauty, their rich, succulent scent, their innocently unfolding buds.

Eric walked over to one of the bushes and began to carefully inspect each flower. "You remember the Rose Crown?"

"Yes," she breathed, kneeling down and inhaling the calming perfume of one of the pink blossoms before glancing at Eric curiously, a prompt for him to continue.

"Would you like me to tell you the story of how the rose crown came to be?"

She nodded, eyes gleaming.

"Long ago, there was a Mira queen, Liv, and a king, Hashim, eldest son of Chryselda Sofia the Red, and they ruled together in Loz. Hashim brought her here to the garden often, for it reminded her of her home, of her people, and she said it held sad yet fond memories for her.

"One day, as they sat in this very clearing, he wove for her a crown of different colored roses. First, a white rose—"

Eric gently cut a white rose from the bush with his pocket knife.

"—which stood for the purity of their love. Next, a yellow rose—"

Here he selected a rose hanging from a low branch of one of the trees, snipping it off as well.

"—which reflected their everlasting friendship, and finally, a red rose—"

He chose a red rose, clipping it from the bush.

"—which was their eternal love and passion.

"And from them, he wove a crown which he set upon her head..."

Eric chose several more white, yellow, and red blossoms and sat beside Chasmira upon the soft grass. She watched intently as he began to weave the roses together, knitting them ever so carefully. She then blushed as he set them upon her head, continuing, "After they married, on the day they were crowned king and queen of Loz, as Liv's cousin, Chrissy, set the crown upon her head, the roses transformed to solid white, yellow, and rose gold. It was a gift from the Mira to Iridescence, for they were honored Hashim had chosen the Lady Liv to be his wife and that their peoples joined together in so beautiful a union."

Eric's eyes shone brightly and deeply into hers. "And now, as a descendent of Liv, you shall someday wear the true Rose Crown. But, for now, this one shall have to suffice."

"I think I prefer this one anyways."

He returned her smile, and for some moments, they sat in the still silence which was interrupted only by the fluttering rhythms of their hearts, those excited pulsations she was almost certain he could hear, those palpitations which increased in excitement, in rapidity, in uneven bounds and leaps as he leaned closer, his cool breath caressing her face, his bottom lip brushing hers...

She jerked away then looked down, embarrassed at her hasty reaction.

"I'm sorry, Eric," she whispered. "I'm just not ready."

"It's okay." He really made it sound as though it truly was.

"Come." He took her hand, helping her to her feet. "Tell me what you'd like to do—we can go anywhere you'd like to go in the garden, anywhere at all."

For some moments, she hesitated, scanning his expression. He really didn't seem offended by her reaction though, so she smiled. "The Endless Lights. I'd like to see those."

He frowned, looking almost frustrated, "Not there, Chasmira. You *know* we can't go there."

"Why not? You said anywhere."

"Yes, but...but they're sacred. Only important people...fairies, prophets, and the like go there."

"But it's not forbidden—"

"The falls. Why don't we see the Falls?"

She hesitated again, considering his reaction. Perhaps he really *had* been hurt by her resistance, only trying not to show it.

"Okay, the Falls sound great."

He showed her the Falls, the lily gardens, the Scintillate Gardens, the Sallie Gardens. They explored every nook and cranny of the garden, save the inner sanctum of the Endless Lights. When lunch arrived, a Mira man brought them a picnic lunch, and when supper came, the same occurred. Eric said he planned it all that way just for her, and when night fell and the first stars began to rise, he asked if she would like to sleep right there in the garden, and she very enthusiast-ically agreed.

So, as night descended, they made their way back to the rose clearing where he spread out a blanket and laid beside her, sliding his arm around her. This token of protective affection she did not resist, for it felt good, right, and safe.

"I love you, Chasmira." His breath tickled her ear, and she snuggled closer against him.

CHAPTER 13

It was not long before his steady snoring signified he was asleep. But Chasmira remained wide awake, her mind whirring with all she'd seen, and, stirring in the back of her mind, the Endless Lights. She half-heartedly tried to push them back, but they soon spiraled to the forefront of her thoughts.

"Chasmira..."

She jumped as the young man called her name in a voice foreign yet echoing with a strange familiarity.

"Chasmira..."

And this time, with it, a dim yet unneglectable flash of white light.

"Chasmira..."

Her heart quickened so fiercely she feared Eric might hear its beat and awaken. When he slept soundly on, she carefully removed his heavy, limp arm from about her waist, and, standing ever so carefully, trod noiselessly upon the plush grass. Drawing the shawl he gave her closely about her shoulders, she tiptoed through the bushes, only to find, on the other side of the clearing, the hedge wall. It stretched up high and magnificently foreboding yet beckoning, like some challenge to be conquered.

"Chasmira..."

Then the light, flashing, this time more brightly from beyond the other side, calling to her in more ways than one, in ways she could not resist...

She walked around the wall's perimeter, feeling until she came to a door, and, reaching out a curious hand, turned the handle and slipped inside.

She shielded her eyes as the pure, white light flooded up from the undecipherable foot of the steps stretching downward before her. Slowly and carefully, she tread down the stone stairs, forced to close her eyes yet feeling no pain from the overpowering light. A moment later, she passed through. She opened her eyes. The Garden of Endless Lights scrolled before her.

"Chasmira..."

The familiar yet unknown voice lurked closer now, though she could no better tell who it might belong to. She walked forth, following its intermittent call and steady blazes of white brilliance until she stopped at last before one of the hovering discs which echoed powerfully, "Chasmira!" Then the vision within the disc took form, and she stared carefully. At first, all was a blur. Then, gradually, the picture formed. She saw herself standing in the phoenix clearing and someone walked up to stand before her, only his figure was made of pure, white light. There was no way of seeing his face, knowing who he was.

"Chasmira..."

The familiarity of the voice echoed more vehemently in her mind, wanting desperately to be heard, to be understood.

The white figure leaned in, pressing her against the tree, kissing her passionately.

Her breath came in struggled fragments even as she watched the same happen to her future self.

Then the vision blurred, and when it cleared again, she was walking towards the throne, only this time, the throne room of the Lozolian Palace was flooded with people. As she looked forward, she could see him, the white figure standing there, looking towards her, waiting. She knew he focused only on her, even though she could not see his face, and especially as he called one last, most tender time,

"Chasmira..."

The vision vanished.

She stood staring, incapable of wrenching away, reaching up a trembling hand to her cheek, touching its wetness. She'd been crying...

Then she turned and hurried towards the garden's door. Eric would worry if he found her missing.

She slipped back into the clearing, under the comfort of his arm, and closed her eyes. Yet she found herself even more restless than before. What was that warm fire surging through her when she beheld the unknown figure, heard the unknown voice, felt his comforting though strange familiarity? Did she at last possess hope of feeling the winter pass from her heart? Of her heart flooding with that same summer flame she most desperately hoped could awaken at Eric's touch? His lips against hers—how foreign they felt, how wrong when he tried to kiss her earlier. She always reserved her first kiss for Aaron. But now, did that vision of the future give her the hope she hardly dared to let live?

She held onto that hope as she snuggled closer to Eric, clutching something soft and another something round and smooth in her pocket, letting the fire fill her as the vivid memory of that small yet not insignificant vision inundated her mind, her heart, her very soul.

CHAPTER 14

When Chasmira awoke, she lay beneath the soft, warm covers of the Palace's bed. She did not stir, save to glance over at the sage, aqua, and lilac butterflies fluttering freely about her curtains. And yet, by the few threads connecting them to the curtain itself, they were not free.

She sighed, and a tear slipped down her cheek. Even in her dreams, the visions of last night did not wane, did not falter. Constant flashes of Aaron, then Eric, then one man whose face was divided, equally displaying their features on either half, reflecting the divide in her heart, a divide she did not know how to cross, to seal, to make whole. Until now. She must choose. She must choose to try to go forward with Eric or else remain in the shadows of Aaron's memory forever.

She slid the bracelet from her wrist with trembling fingers but then clutched it tightly, so tightly it burned, cut into her palm. She *had* to let it go, didn't she? But how *could* she? Such an act was unfathomably traitorous, blasphemous...

A soft knock on the door. Eric's voice saying, "Chasmira, love, are you up yet?"

She glanced at the sun. She'd slept late. The dreams held her back from waking.

"Chasmira?"

Taking in a staggering breath, she plunged the bracelet deep into her pocket, alongside the feather and pearl.

"Chasmira, are you alright?"

She released it. The tears washed over her. Yet she found strength to say, "Yes, I'm fine, I'll be there in a minute."

"I hope I didn't wake you, I was only concerned, since it's so late—"

"No, I'm fine, you're fine." She slid from the bed, walking over to the wardrobe, fighting back the tears as she began to prepare for the day, quickly. Tears had no place here. They mustn't. Not those tears. Not anymore.

She changed swiftly, brushing her hair smooth. And then, with a final breath, she turned towards the sunlit door and prepared to face a new day.

117

THE AMIELIAN LEGACY

The Stregoni Sequence *(Four-book collection)*

The Chronicles of the Mira

The Hero Chronicles *(Five-book collection)*

The Gailean Quartet *(Four-book collection)*

Loz *(Three-book collection)*

The Legends of Surprisers Series *(Three-book collection)*

The Pirates of Meleeon

The Crystal Rings

Bloodmaiden

Lily in the Snow and Other Elemental Tales

Chimes, La Mariposa: Two Tales of Emreal

The Last Star

StarChild

Follow Me

Black Lace

The Boy Who Fell From the Sky

Tears of a Vampire Prince: the First Krystine *(A companion to The Stregoni Sequence)*

Carousel in the Clouds

THE HERO CHRONICLES

THE HERO OF 1000 YEARS

HEROES REUNITED

HEROES OF THE DOVE

THE SECRET SISTER AND THE SILVER KNIGHT

THE PRINCESS OF DESTINY AND THE PRINCESS OF THE NIGHT

Made in the USA
Charleston, SC
23 May 2012